*Also by Cora Harrison from Severn House*

*The Gaslight mysteries*

SEASON OF DARKNESS
WINTER OF DESPAIR
SUMMER OF SECRETS
SPRING OF HOPE

*The Reverend Mother mysteries*

A SHAMEFUL MURDER
A SHOCKING ASSASSINATION
BEYOND ABSOLUTION
A GRUESOME DISCOVERY
DEATH OF A NOVICE
MURDER AT THE QUEEN'S OLD CASTLE
DEATH OF A PROMINENT CITIZEN
MURDER IN AN ORCHARD CEMETERY
MURDER IN THE CATHEDRAL
THE DEADLY WEED

*The Burren mysteries*

WRIT IN STONE
EYE OF THE LAW
SCALES OF RETRIBUTION
DEED OF MURDER
LAWS IN CONFLICT
CHAIN OF EVIDENCE
CROSS OF VENGEANCE
VERDICT OF THE COURT
CONDEMNED TO DEATH
A FATAL INHERITANCE
AN UNJUST JUDGE

T0265717

# MURDER IN THE MIST

# MURDER IN THE MIST

## Cora Harrison

**SEVERN
HOUSE**

First world edition published in Great Britain and the USA in 2023
by Severn House, an imprint of Canongate Books Ltd,
14 High Street, Edinburgh EH1 1TE.

severnhouse.com

*British Library Cataloguing-in-Publication Data*
A CIP catalogue record for this title is available from the British Library.

ISBN-13: 978-1-4483-1134-7 (cased)
ISBN-13: 978-1-4483-1135-4 (e-book)

*All Severn House titles are printed on acid-free paper.*

MIX
Paper from
responsible sources
FSC
www.fsc.org   FSC® C013056

Typeset by Palimpsest Book Production Ltd.,
Falkirk, Stirlingshire, Scotland.
Printed and bound in Great Britain by
TJ Books, Padstow, Cornwall.

# Praise for the Gaslight mysteries

# About the author

**Cora Harrison** turned to writing historical fiction after she retired from teaching to live on a farm near the Burren in the west of Ireland. As well as the Gaslight mysteries, she is the author of the Reverend Mother mysteries, and the Mara series of Celtic mysteries, set in 16th century Ireland.

www.coraharrison.com

# ACKNOWLEDGEMENTS

A serious illness while in the latter stages of this book meant that I owe a huge debt of gratitude to those who helped me to bring it to its conclusion. So, even more than usual, I want to thank my agent, Peter Buckman; editors Anna Harrisson, Mary Karayel and the other members of Severn House's editorial staff who, well above the call of duty, have come to my rescue and enabled the book to be finished on time.

I am hugely grateful to all.

# PROLOGUE

I, Wilkie Collins, acclaimed author of *The Woman in White* (and of the slightly less well-known book, *The Moonstone*), have often, surreptitiously, wondered whether I would have been more acclaimed and far better known if I had been born in a different era to the author Charles Dickens. There were many good writers in this second half of the nineteenth century, but all of us, I think, were eclipsed by the great Charles Dickens. Nevertheless, I endeavoured to suppress these feelings of envy and to profit as much as possible from my friendship with the great man. I asked his advice frequently and in spare minutes from my own work I had begun to write down as much as possible about his lifestyle, his ideas on writing literature and his memories of triumphal progress through the cities and counties of the British Isles. I wrote to him continuously whenever he was on his travels and he, wonderful man that he was, never failed to write back, no matter how busy he was. And that was how I heard all the details about his visit to Ireland.

It had been a huge success! His first visit was to Dublin, the capital city. Not a seat unoccupied. Not a dry eye in the hall when he read the terrible scene about the death of poor Nancy. And the same successes in Belfast and in Limerick. It was Cork city, however, which was the place that took his fancy. He liked its position surrounded by hills and tapering into the ocean from the multitude of rivers, but it was the people that he loved, their warmth, their excitement, and the music of their sing-song voices. He wrote to tell me, triumphantly, that while the expensive seats in the Cork Atheneum were, of course, all filled without exception, the cheap seats mostly held two to three, with hefty farmers sitting on top of each other and children perched on top of shoulders. The Atheneum made a fortune that night, according to Dickens.

Cork was the last city in Ireland where he visited and Cork was where, for the first time, that he accepted private hospitality, first to visit the seaside port of Queenstown from where so many Irish set off to America, and a few days later an invitation to dinner by a hospitable lady who intrigued his imagination with tales about Blarney Castle and its wonderful stone.

And it was there that he met Timmy O'Connor and his nephews.

My Dear Wilkie,

Talk about the famous Irish hospitality! No sooner had I expressed interest when told, over the dinner table, the story of the magical stone in the walls of Blarney Castle and of how those who kissed it were endowed with the gift of eloquence for the rest of their lives, than one of the guests, a man named Timmy O'Connor, jumped to his feet, abandoning a plateful of the most delicious pudding and abruptly left the room. When he was gone the rest of the guests, in a true Cork fashion, vied with each other to relate stories about this man, a bit of a ne'er-do-well, by all accounts, in both England and Ireland, but a source of great amusement to his neighbours, judging by the gales of laughter as they told stories about how he outwitted the law in both countries – 'but a great man to do you a favour' – most of the stories about this man ended up with those words.

And, sure enough, Timmy O'Connor lived up to expectations on that night. As soon as coffee had been consumed, there was a loud sound of a hunting horn, blown at full throttle, and there, outside the window, was the man himself, accompanied by his four nephews, Swayne, Caleb, Tiffen and Bypers, all sitting on top of the traditional Irish jaunting car – an enormously long cart, drawn by a team of horses.

And, of course the whole party joined into the fun. I, and as many others who could fit, were seated on the jaunting car. More horses and carts were produced and the whole party set off for Blarney Castle singing at the tops of voices. Bottles of poteen (an illicit Irish brew, stronger, my dear Wilkie, than any whiskey I have ever consumed), were passed around and I pondered a plan to be the last man of the whole company to kiss this famous stone and perhaps manage to evade it completely as I began to understand that it involved bending back-wards over the top of the castle wall while hanging on to an iron bar.

I put the proposal to Timmy, explaining that I would profit from watching the performance of the authentic Cork natives and was met with a grin. 'Lord love you, Mr Dickens, sure, Cork people never kiss the stone. We're all born with the gift of the gab! We'd lose it if we kissed the stone! Have another swig of the whiskey and you won't even notice yourself doing it.'

And, so, my dear Wilkie, I had to kiss the Blarney Stone while Timmy O'Connor, stout fellow that he was, held my two ankles in such a firm grip of iron that it reassured me as I clutched the bars, lowered my head and shoulders down the wall and imprinted a hasty kiss on the famous stone. Never did whiskey taste so good as that homemade brew when I swallowed some down after I was pulled back up to safety.

In fact, I was so relieved, and my mood was so cheerful, that I ended by inviting the entire company, Timmy, and his four nephews, to come and visit me in Gad's Hill if they were ever in the south-east of England! Let's hope they don't take me at my word!

Your affectionate friend,
Charles Dickens

I read his letter with enjoyment and put it carefully in the box where I kept everything to do with Charles Dickens. Little did I think that I, myself, would ever meet Timmy O'Connor. And I certainly never thought that the man's name would be engraved upon my memory.

But I did meet him and will never forget the name. And this was how it happened.

It must have been about some time in the middle of

December when I received the invitation from my friend,
Charles Dickens, to spend Christmas with himself, his family
and his friends at Gad's Hill, his Kentish country home. It
was an immensely welcome invitation and immediately, for
the first time since my boyhood, I began to look forward to
Christmas.

I had, I must say, already received a grudging Christmas
invitation from my mother with the sour postscript: 'As I have
plenty of domestic staff, please do *not* bring your housekeeper
and her daughter!'

That had done nothing to kindle a Christmas spirit within
me; nothing, except to irritate me. In my mother's letter the
word before 'housekeeper' had been crossed out – but
crossed out with just a single line so narrow as to allow the
word 'mistress' to be easily read. I put the missive in
the fire and decided that my mother had no affection for me
if she could not see how happy I was with Caroline and her
daughter, little Carrie.

And so, the invitation from Dickens was doubly
heart-warming:

> My dear Wilkie,
>     Christmas is my favourite time of the year, and it will
> be doubly pleasant if you and your family are here in
> Gad's Hill, celebrating the Christmas season with us.
>     Do bring Caroline and, of course, my little friend 'the
> Butler'. Both are very welcome. My youngest, Plorn, is
> a similar age to Carrie and they will have 'great larks'
> together!

Caroline's daughter, little Carrie, was a great favourite with
Dickens and he had given her the nickname of 'the Butler'
since the time when she hid under the dinner table and emerged
with the excuse of an offer of a second helping of pudding at
his elbow when the conversation became interesting to her.

'Why, please my soul, it's the Butler,' had said Dickens,
always one to be fond of children. And, from then onwards,
little Carrie was known to him and to other friends as 'the
Butler'.

# ONE

Since Caroline had already received an invitation from her sister in Essex, I happily accepted Dickens' invitation for myself and 'the Butler' – much to the child's huge delight, and a couple of days before Christmas we two, Carrie and myself, took the train from London into Kent. I easily filled the boredom of the journey by describing to her, in as much detail as I could manage, Dickens' country home with its two fields, the horses, the dogs, the parrot, the big cupboard full of toys and, very exciting, the underground passageway where she and Dickens' sons could run beneath the road from one of his fields to the other one across the road.

He was the most hospitable of men, Charles Dickens, and so I was not surprised, when the train from London stopped at Higham station, to see a carriage with a group of people waiting for us.

I recognized Dickens' carriage as I knew the man who advanced to meet us. He was William Wills, Dickens' friend, and the sub-editor of Dickens' magazine, *Household Words*, and so I went across and chatted with him. He remembered little Carrie; remembered, also, Dickens' nickname for her and then introduced me to the other four men who were with him, each bearing the Irish surname of O'Connor: one a middle-aged man, Timmy O'Connor; and the other three, his nephews, who appeared to be in their early twenties. Irish, by their accents, I thought, but it was only when I heard the slightly odd names of the nephews – Swayne, Bypers and Caleb – that I remembered Dickens' account of his visit to Cork. I told them I had heard all about Dickens' trip to Ireland and I enquired about the famous Blarney Stone and that I had heard from Dickens that it brought luck to anyone who kissed it, but that Cork people did not have to kiss it.

'Perhaps we should have kissed the Blarney Stone before we left Ireland,' said Caleb. 'We've had nothing but bad luck since we came over. My twin brother, Tiffen, broke his leg getting down a wagon and he is still in hospital in the town of Rochester, in fact we have just come back from visiting him.'

I expressed my sympathy, of course, but was quickly interrupted by the older man.

'You are forgetting something, Caleb; you haven't mentioned Mr Dickens' kindness in inviting us to stay in his house so that poor Tiffen should not be left alone in a foreign country during the season of Christmas,' said his uncle in a reproving tone, addressing his nephew in a manner more appropriate to a child rather than a young man. In fact, the situation embarrassed me so much, especially when I saw the anger on the younger man's face, that I launched into a description of Dickens' kindness and hospitality to his friends and got myself in a muddle, until Wills, taking pity on me, called for two volunteers to walk the steep hill ahead of us. Caleb immediately volunteered and so did I, but then remembered Carrie who would, undoubtedly, make a big fuss if I deserted her.

'I'm afraid that I have to look after the little one,' I said regretfully. And that had the desired effect as Carrie immediately declared that she was a very big girl, who could look after herself and that a walk would do me good. She bounced up onto the wagon beside Wills and began to interrogate him about the news of Santa Claus, and soon he was occupying Carrie's attention with a long story of how he heard that Santa Claus with his sack of toys had been seen in the sky around a corner near to Mr Dickens' house. Caleb and I were then free to set out at a steep pace.

'I'm very sorry to hear the misfortune about your brother and his broken leg,' I said.

He gave me a rather odd look. 'According to my uncle, it's a piece of the most extraordinary good luck. The whole of Ireland will get to know how we spent Christmas in the house of the famous Charles Dickens.'

I was embarrassed, but at the same time curious. 'You don't like your uncle much, do you?' I said, and my voice was purposely light-hearted, as though I had received his words as some sort of joke. Caleb then proceeded to tell me why they were there at Dickens' house and to give me some background to his family.

Timmy was the name of the older man, uncle to the younger men. They had all come over from Ireland for the funeral of a very elderly aunt of his who had lived in London and who had no other relative left alive except himself her nephew and the four younger siblings. These young men were the sons of Timmy's dead brother Patrick, and were, I thought, as I got to know them, as different and as unusual as their names.

Swayne was the eldest – a heavily-built young man with a bushy, very black beard, dark brown eyes, and a pair of the largest hands which I had ever seen. He was a carpenter, he told us – a carpenter who had ambition to set up his own business, building timber summer houses along the picturesque coastline of County Cork for wealthy clients. Timber, apparently, lasted very well in the mild wet climate of Ireland and as the houses would only be used during the summer, there would be little difficulty in heating them. They could be cheaply built and rented out every summer for a good weekly sum. If he had some capital to buy the timber, well . . . he would make a fortune, the young man's brother confided in me.

'What a good idea,' I said enthusiastically to Swayne, who was sitting along with his uncle in the carriage, but I was interrupted by Timmy who had overheard our conversation. He laughed heartily and told me that it was easily to be seen that I knew as little as his nephew about what people wanted from a house.

'No brains, that fellow,' he said, and I tried to cover up the rude statement by expressing an interest in these 'summer chalets' as Swayne had named them and asked for more details. I noticed how low Swayne's voice was as he struggled to reply to my questions and how from time to time he glanced uneasily at his uncle. I began to take a dislike to the man. Why was he so set on criticizing his nephew. In fact, he ridiculed him so much that, after a few moments, Swayne fell silent and sat twisting his large hands together as his uncle Timmy laid down the law about what people wanted from a house.

After enduring a few more minutes, we were thankfully

back on the flat track and were encouraged to sit back again in the carriage. This gave me the opportunity to hastily interrupt O'Connor with a request for the names of the other young men in his family, and so 'Uncle Timmy' turned his attention to his other nephews.

The second was Bypers, as small and thin in frame as his older brother was large – a six-month child, according to his uncle, who roared with laughter as he announced that Bypers had been trying to catch up on his brother for most of his life but failing most miserably. Bypers, I noticed, winced as though this was a joke which he had heard all too often. He was a clerk in an office and was so small that I wondered how he could climb on a stool. He was, said his uncle, always wasting time, painting pictures of the rough seas along the Cork coastline. I listened with interest to this. My own dear father, now deceased, I told him encouragingly, had been an artist and he had made a fortune by selling his paintings of stormy seas. They became so popular that furniture shops stocked various examples and soon it became the fashion to have a 'Collins Sea-View' painting in all fashionable houses and my father began to sell each painting as soon as it was finished and even had a waiting list of new orders to hand. My father had, I told him, made a large enough fortune from his paintings to have given our family a very easy and pleasant livelihood during his lifetime and he had left my mother, my brother and myself in extremely comfortable circumstances after his death.

I thought it would encourage Bypers to hear this, but his uncle, who was listening, assured me that his nephew, unlike my father, probably, was no good at painting and that, in any case, there was no possibility that he would ever get the energy to persuade people to buy his daubs. 'Messy-looking things' was his verdict on Bypers' paintings, and he was equally scathing about his nephew who he said had no brains and, unlike my father, he assured me, no ability to talk people into buying his pictures. When Bypers tried to tell me about the scenery along the West Cork coastline, he rudely interrupted him, telling his nephew that I would have no interest in 'back-of-beyond' places such as West Cork.

And then there was Caleb, with his absent twin Tiffen, the third and fourth brothers, tall, strong-looking, silent, and very self-possessed. Caleb was, according to his uncle, one of these half-wits who stuck his head in a book and when he came out of it had nothing to say. Caleb grimaced and muttered that he, himself, wanted to write a book but was tied to this job of being a solicitor's clerk and had no energy left over after a day's work. He got a certain courage from my expression of interest, I think, and informed me that he almost felt like giving up his ambition to write a book, unless, he said, someone would encourage him by telling him that what he wrote was worthwhile. He looked shyly at Dickens' editor when he disclosed his ambition, but Wills, though a kind-hearted man, ignored him. Dickens had heard too much from people who wanted to write a book and who would certainly write a book if they had the time and leisure! The last thing our host would want – I knew this as well as did Wills – was a would-be writer buttonholing him on every possible occasion during the Christmas festive season and looking for useful tips and encouragement. However, I promised myself that I would have some helpful conversations with the poor fellow. My own two published books were beginning to do well, and I congratulated myself with the thought that I had invented a new genre – this combination of a story, an exciting murder, and a puzzle for the reader to identify the murderer.

I was new to the world of authors – so new, in fact, that the sight of a bookshop window displaying one or both of my two books brought a rush of warm excitement to me and ensured that I spend a good five minutes lingering in front of the shop window and hoping for someone to comment upon the books there. And so, I was happy to talk about the process to anyone who would listen to me. I was aware that Dickens had given me so many helpful hints when I was writing *The Woman in White* that he had helped me to produce what I felt to be a polished and well-written book. Now, perhaps, I could pass on some of his valuable advice to someone else who was as badly in need of it as I had been when I first met Dickens. Still the atmosphere in the crowded cab was wrong for a serious conversation. I smiled at Caleb in a friendly fashion, told him that we must have a long conversation together during the Christmas holiday break, but then turned my attention to questioning his brothers.

Tiffen, twin brother to Caleb – and uncannily alike to him, I was assured, worked in an engineering firm. He was, apparently, a cyclist; he owned a penny-farthing bike and had a brilliant idea, which his brother Caleb related to us, interrupted with noises of derision and shouts of laughter by his uncle, an invention which involved putting an engine onto the big wheel of the bicycle, to be powered by motion of the wheel at the early stages of the cycle ride and then this engine could be switched at the later stages of the cycle ride and so the cyclist could travel all day without exhausting himself.

'Thinks that he will make a fortune,' said his uncle with a chuckle. 'All he needs is some fool to invest his money in him. And to convince the public that they want an ugly great lump of an engine attached to the front wheel of a bicycle.' He shot a glance at the downcast faces of his nephews and laughed uproariously. Caleb looked at him uneasily but said nothing. It seemed extraordinary to me, that these nephews, all grown men, appeared to be afraid of their unpleasant uncle. Full of fear and of hatred, I thought, looking uneasily at the faces of the nephews as they listened to the outbreak of malicious laughter from their uncle.

'You shouldn't laugh at him,' said my little Carrie reprovingly. 'Bicycles are good. I'd like a bicycle for my birthday.' She gave me a look to make sure that I was listening and then said in a stage whisper to Caleb, 'I've been talking and talking about wanting a bicycle and now I'll keep talking about a bicycle with an engine so that I can go really fast and get away from the grown-up people.'

'I'm not listening,' I said jokingly, thinking, not for the first time, that a chatterbox like Carrie was a great asset in an embarrassing situation such as this awkward position that Timothy O'Connor had created with his unpleasant words about his nephews. Luckily that proved to be true on this occasion as everyone seized on Carrie's words with alacrity and began talking about Christmas presents and bringing up recollections of the past. Even the unpleasant uncle chimed in with a few memories. I left them to their recollections and deliberately moved to a seat next to Caleb.

'I was in your position a few years ago,' I told him, speaking in an undertone. 'I was supposed to be studying to be a barrister, but all that I really wanted to do was to write books. I'm afraid I rather neglected my studies,' I continued as I saw how interested he was and added, 'but at the same time, because I had a certain amount of work to do and lectures to attend, and because, I suppose, that I didn't want to disappoint my dear, kind father, well . . . I made poor progress. The law was a distraction even though I wasn't really doing enough work to pass any examination.'

I didn't like to think of how stupid and what a timewaster that I had been during those years and so I hurried to complete my story. 'However,' I went on rapidly, 'as soon as my father died, things were different. I came in for a good legacy from my father. That gave me the opportunity I was waiting for and so I ceased to study the law and I devoted as much time as I possibly could, day and night, to my first novel, *The Woman in White*. Luckily it was a success,' I told him. 'My next book, *The Moonstone*, is also doing well so that now I hope to make a permanent living from my pen.'

Caleb's face lit up. 'I envy you,' he said and then, in a low tone, he continued, speaking softly into my ear, 'and I must say that I had hoped that I too might have had similar luck. My dear old aunt in London, the lady who has just died, well, whenever we visited her, she had been most interested in the book which I was trying to write and she did promise . . .' He lowered his voice almost to a whisper, and continued, 'Well, she certainly hinted that I might get good news some time when she was no longer around. Not that I wished her death,' he added hastily, 'but she was ninety-seven years old and bedridden, so the news of her death came as no surprise. In fact, my uncle went over there a few weeks ago when the nurse phoned him to say that she could not live too long, but . . .'

'She had not made a will, I suppose,' I said sympathetically.

'Yes, she had.' Caleb's mouth tightened. He stared over the

head of the coachman for a moment, then lowering his voice and looking at me meaningfully, he said, 'As I told you, my uncle had visited her a month before her death and had, quite rightly, I suppose, urged her to make a will. And she did. He arranged for the solicitor to call with two witnesses. It was all done properly.'

He stopped abruptly and I waited for the conclusion, but when he said no more, I said in a low voice, 'Don't tell me! She left all her money to him.'

Caleb compressed his lips. For a moment, he said nothing, but then he shrugged his shoulders. 'All was quite legally done as I said. The will was drawn up by the solicitor and witnessed by his clerk and by the nurse who attended her. The only beneficiary was her nearest relative, her nephew, Timmy my uncle.' He shrugged his shoulders, again. 'Made sense, I suppose,' he said. 'He was a nearer relative than any of us brothers who were just sons of a nephew who had died almost twenty years ago.'

I opened my mouth to sympathize, but then shut it as I noticed that, although we had been speaking quietly, Uncle Timothy's pale green eyes were fixed upon us and were narrowed into an expression of suspicion. I bent over Carrie and called her attention to a red-breasted robin who was pecking at a bush beside the road and by the time that I lifted my head again, Timothy was talking in an undertone to Dickens' friend, Wills.

'You don't think that your uncle will share any of the bounty with you, do you?' I questioned Caleb in a low tone.

'Not likely,' he added, with a look across the carriage at his Uncle Timmy who seemed unconcerned, looking hale and hearty as he roared with laughter at something said by Wills. 'Not likely,' he repeated with a little more confidence, although his voice was still lowered. 'Mind you, there was a time when I thought that I would convince him that my father would have wished me to make use of my talent, but . . .' Caleb paused for a moment and then said with forced cheerfulness, 'But, who knows what the future will bring! I may be as lucky as you.'

I felt a pang of guilt that I had implied that the death of

my very loved father had been a stroke of luck. Nevertheless, I was sorry for the man with his sensitive and rather unhappy face.

'You think that you, too, may get a legacy at some stage,' I said, speaking, as he did, quite softly and with my mouth near to his ear as the iron wheels of the carriage clattered over the stony road.

Caleb said nothing for a moment; he cast a look at his brothers and his uncle and then said in a low tone, 'My uncle has said that he made a will leaving all that he possesses to be divided between us all. It's the truth. He invited us to check with his solicitor. I think because Tiffen challenged him over my aunt's will – we were so sure that she was leaving her money to us – and so my uncle, I suppose to stop Tiffen who can be the bravest of us all, brought us to his solicitor and got him to show us the copy of his "Last Will and Testament" as he kept calling it. He has left his money to be evenly divided between us.'

'So, you will have the means to devote yourself to your art one day,' I said as encouragingly as I could. However, it was a poor hope, I thought. The uncle of these four young men appeared to be not more than twenty-five to thirty or so years older than his nephews. They would have to wait a long time before they inherited the promised money.

'It's my only hope,' said Caleb. 'I don't think I have any other rich relations who could leave me some money and, sadly, I have nothing of my own.' He hesitated for a moment and then lowered his voice even more – almost whispering into my ear as he started to tell me the story of his life.

'We had a strange upbringing, my brothers and myself,' he said. 'My father and mother died when we were quite young. My father was a rich man and, although quite a young man at his death, he had left a will leaving everything to my mother but specifying that in the event of her predeceasing him, or dying at the same time as her husband, that all which he possessed was to be used in the upbringing and schooling of his four sons. He hoped that one of his brothers would take over the task and bequeathed all of which he possessed for our care and for our education to that brother who would sign a deed to say that he would take care of us. Otherwise, if none of his brothers volunteered, then the money was to be used by his solicitor and we were to be sent to boarding school. Well, my Uncle Timmy took the money and took over the care of us, but as he was not married and showed no warmth and little interest in us, we had a bleak upbringing – a cheap boarding school and then a pair of servants and a tutor to look after us in a hired house, during the holidays. The house was always the cheapest that he could find and never by the sea or in a pleasant location. And when we left school, there was, apparently, no money left over to pay to send us to university or to train us in a worthwhile profession.'

Caleb stopped abruptly as at that moment his uncle got up from his seat and came to sit beside us on the pretext of looking at the view from our side of the carriage.

I thought that my new friend was in an unfortunate position and that his father must have been a gullible man whose early death proved to be a tragedy in more ways than one for his four sons. Nevertheless, I knew that I should be discreet and so quickly engaged 'Uncle Timmy' in conversation.

'How kind of Mr Dickens to invite you to stay with him at Gad's Hill. Had you arranged to meet him whilst over in England, then?' I asked him, remembering that Dickens had only offered an invitation out of politeness when they'd been in Cork, never expecting it to be followed up on – and at Christmas too!

'He invited us to visit him when we met him in Cork,' said Uncle Timmy proudly, 'so we did, and then that foolish nephew of mine went and broke his leg, but Mr Dickens, well bless my soul, didn't Mr Charles Dickens take out his card, write down instructions on how to reach his house, and invite the whole lot of us to spend a few days over Christmas with him and his family and friends! Couldn't believe our ears, could we, lads?' he said to his nephews and without waiting for an answer told me the rest of the story. 'And so, once we were sure that he was serious, and we had enquired whether his good lady would mind having all these extra guests . . .'

'What did he say to that?' I enquired, supressing a grin. Dickens, I knew, was the person who ruled that household and his wife, Catherine, was always only too eager to please him in any way.

'Didn't even mention her name – brushed it aside. He's the boss of the household, I would reckon!' Uncle Timmy gave a knowing grin before adding, 'Said he always tried to fill the house at Christmas, and that he had plenty of servants who enjoyed having a crowd of people to look after. Told us to come on the day before Christmas Eve and that he would guarantee us a merry Christmas. He was so pressing that we gave in immediately and accepted his invitation so here we are – chance of a lifetime – going to spend Christmas with Charles Dickens. The whole of Cork city will hear about this!' He bounced up and down with pleasure at the thought of how he could impress his friends and neighbours.

'You're squashing me,' said Carrie petulantly. 'Why don't you go and sit over there. You'd have one big seat all for yourself.'

'Carrie!' I exclaimed reprovingly, but Timmy just grimaced and moved away with a perfunctory wave of his hand. He didn't say anything, but when I saw his face, I felt embarrassed. He had flushed a dark red and his lips were compressed into a narrow tight line. He was obviously furious. I shrugged my shoulders. After all, it was in fact more than a bit ridiculous to take notice of what a five-year-old said. Most people were indulgent towards Carrie who was a pretty child with a charming smile most of the time. She was tired now, I thought, as I saw her scowl, so I directed my attention towards amusing her on the journey, pointing out a squirrel that scrambled up a bare-leaved oak tree and another cheerful, red-breasted robin which now flew after our carriage.

I was conscious, as I strove to entertain a tired little girl, that my voice was the only one to be heard in the carriage. At the hint of anger from their uncle, all the nephews had immediately ceased to speak and occupied themselves with looking out at the countryside with unsmiling faces. Not a good feeling among these visitors, I told myself and hoped that the hospitality and exuberant atmosphere of Dickens' country home would lighten the atmosphere once we arrived at Gad's Hill.

Dickens had bought this house of Gad's Hill and the land around it on an impulse, meaning to let out the house and thus provide himself and his large family with a steady income during a year when book sales were erratic. However, Gad's Hill proved to be the ideal outlet for his hospitable nature and soon this idea was jettisoned, and the house was furnished and staffed and filled full of guests from one end of the year to the other. The house was relatively old-fashioned – a couple of hundred years old, I guessed – and it was a three-storey building made from red brick, with a bell turret on the roof and a wooden porch in front of it. He would, I reckoned, own the fields around it and when he first bought the place, he had been full of stories about the games of cricket and football all of which he expected his guests to join in with enthusiasm. I would, I decided, when I spotted football goal posts, make Carrie an excuse to get out of all forms of forced exercise and jollifications.

'She'll be such a nuisance to you,' had been her mother's verdict. 'Why on earth do you have to keep giving in to her? She shouldn't be allowed to rule the roost at her age! Let her come with me to my sister's place and she can help to mind the baby,' said Caroline.

'She doesn't want to go to your sister's house,' I said. 'She says that she doesn't like babies,' I added.

'That's because you spoil her, and she wants to be the most important person in the house. She doesn't like playing second fiddle to the baby,' said Carrie's mother.

I shrugged. It was probably true, but why shouldn't the child be allowed to choose. I wasn't too keen on babies myself.

'I can't change arrangements now,' I told her. 'Dickens asked for her to come. She can play with his younger boys – she's just about the same age as his youngest boy, Plorn. Anyway, he's expecting her. It's all fixed.'

But now, looking at Carrie's sulky face, I began to wish that I had listened to her mother. None of the other guests looked as if they would share my child-minding duties – in fact once the cloud came over their uncle's face, they all busied themselves with newspapers or magazines and I was left to struggle with a tired and bad-tempered little girl. Would I be burdened with her for the whole of the Christmas break?

But, of course, I should have known Dickens better. Though for ever complaining about the size of his family and the expense and trouble that they put him to, Dickens was, at heart, a great child lover and when he decided to put on a show for children, it was done to perfection, down to the last detail. As the carriage came nearer to the red brick building that was Gad's Hill, I could hear voices singing Christmas carols. My little Carrie ceased to sulk and sat up very straight, her eyes shining.

'"Jingle Bells, Jingle Bells",' sang an assortment of voices: young boys' voices, half-broken adolescent voices and a fine strong baritone soaring above them all as the words rose above the hedge. Our carriage stopped, one of the men ran around to hold the horses' heads and the other, with an ear-to-ear smile upon his face, turned to Carrie. 'Shut your eyes, little miss! Be quick! Don't open until I tell you.'

Carrie's face was flushed with excitement. Obediently she shut her eyes tightly, screwing up her little face. The singing became louder, the gate was opened, and at that very moment a figure with a white beard made from cotton wool and dressed in what looked like a fur-edged, red dressing gown, came through the open gate, followed by a troupe of boys dressed as elves.

'Open your eyes, little girl,' said Dickens' voice, deepened to a fair imitation of a pantomime Santa Claus.

'I need another elf and you look to be just what I am looking for,' he added as soon as, with an excited giggle, Carrie opened her eyes and looked wonderingly at the cartload of holly, ivy and costume-wearing boys, the younger half of the Dickens family, all dressed as elves.

'Go with Mrs Santa, and the rest of the elves,' said the elaborately dressed Santa Claus. He lifted Carrie down and without any hesitation she went off, holding the hand of Mrs Santa who I guessed to be the governess who looked after Dickens' youngest sons and who made a good start by telling Carrie that there was an elf's costume all ready for her and lying on her bed in the night nursery. I sat back, grinned, breathed in a sigh of relief and allowed Dickens to greet his Irish guests.

'We, myself and the boys, are putting on a play for you and every one of the guests, tonight,' said Dickens, completely at his ease, despite his Santa Claus costume, greeting each one of his guests by name. He whispered in my ear, 'Don't worry about Carrie. We've put a bed for her in the nursery. Just beside Mrs Santa and the youngest elf, Master Plorn. Names above their beds so that Santa can find them! You can enjoy yourself, Collins, you may sit up all night drinking if you wish.'

I shook his hand thankfully. It had begun to dawn upon me that I had done a stupid thing to take over the sole charge of a self-willed five-year-old girl. However, Dickens' governess was a lady who would be used to handling all those boys and should be able to take care of Carrie. I melted into the background and enjoyed myself with Dickens and his guests, putting Carrie from my mind while I busied myself helping the gang of workers that Dickens had already set to work by cutting branches of holly from an enormous old tree and tearing off long strands of ivy from the stone wall of the field. Meanwhile, Dickens walked his other guests into the house. Charley, Dickens' eldest son, raised an eyebrow at me, and I was happy to explain the arrival of an extra four guests to him.

'Your father had arranged to meet up with them in London for tea, then found out about Tiffen's broken leg and that they would have to spend Christmas in England instead of going back to their home. And so, your father being the man he is, well, he invited them spend Christmas at Gad's Hill,' I explained.

Of course, if the matter had concerned anyone other than Charles Dickens, I would probably have expressed the hope that the lady of the house would not be too upset and annoyed that her arrangements for Christmas were disrupted at such short notice, but anyone with the slightest knowledge of the household knew that it was Dickens, not his wife who ruled the roost in this household. And to give him his due he was the one who would have made all the arrangements, devised all the menus, briefed the servants, and checked the arrangements of each bedroom designated for a guest.

I relaxed and allowed myself to anticipate a wonderful Christmas where everything for the guests' enjoyment would be done in an atmosphere of laughter and harmonious singing and performances of plays not unworthy of London's West End.

# TWO

hoped, as I went to find my hostess, Dickens' amiable wife, Kate, that Swayne, Bypers and Caleb were going to enjoy Christmas as much as I expected to. As for that unpleasant uncle of theirs, well, if he didn't appreciate the spirit of laughter and gaiety that would prevail at Gad's Hill, he always had the thought of that substantial legacy from his recently deceased aunt to keep his spirits at a true Christmas level. I resolved to assist Dickens as much as I could and to ensure that these three ill-treated nephews of that unpleasant man would enjoy a happy and traditional Christmas, perhaps for the very first time in their lives.

Dickens, I realized, during just a short meeting in a London public house, had summed up the relationship between uncle and nephews with the accommodation he had reserved for his guests. The three young men were squashed into one room in an attic at the top of the house – a large one, but still rather overcrowded by the three beds, whereas the uncle had a room of his own in the storey beneath, well away from his nephews. They didn't care how squashed they were, I thought when, on Dickens' instructions, I went to see if they had everything that they needed. They were, however, said Bypers, rather puzzled by the bottle of whiskey and the three small glass tumblers left on a tray on top of one of the chest of drawers.

'Was it left by accident?' he asked me in a troubled fashion, and I quickly assured him that Dickens was the best of hosts and would be delighted to see them enjoy themselves in every respect and that he was a firm believer in providing his guests with the means to make themselves a hot toddy at night or to have a drink after a walk or before coming down to dinner. I advised them to unpack and promised to return to conduct them to the dining room when the bell for dinner went in about an hour's time. And then I left them, looking

furtively at each other. They would, I thought, soon get used
to the absence of that bullying uncle of theirs.

As I turned to go back upstairs to the nursery and check
on Carrie, I met Dickens who stood firmly in the centre of
the stairs and spread out both arms to make a barrier.

'The "Butler" and Plorn are playing happily with his toy
railway, Wilkie, and if you go up now, she will immediately
start crying for her mother or sending you on some impossible
errand,' he said. Then he added, 'Leave her alone. Believe me,
my friend; I'm an expert on children. And I always know the
right thing to do.'

'You're right,' I said humbly.

And, as I expected, he said instantly, 'I'm always right.
Now come along, Wilkie. Be a good fellow and come upstairs
to the schoolroom. I need someone to help me put up the
curtains for the play tonight and a few little jobs like that.'

I hesitated. I knew Dickens when he was in that active mood
of his. Nothing pleased him as much as throwing commands
at anyone whom he managed to enrol as an assistant. Added
to the fact that he was a perfectionist, I could see that I was
in for an unpleasant half hour or so. Not even my most ardent
admirer from among my friends could say that I was of use
when it came to any practical work around a house. And then
I had an inspiration.

'Let's go and find your new guests,' I said hastily. 'They
look to be three strong young fellows. You know me. I'm no
good at that sort of thing. I know I'll make a mess of it.'

Without waiting for his permission, I went hastily up the
flight of stairs and knocked softly at the door. It was opened
instantly by Swayne. He was a carpenter, I remembered, and I
looked with satisfaction at his sturdy frame and large hands.
I could see instantly that I had done the right thing as the
three guests were standing around the room, quite ill-at-ease
and looking as though they had not the slightest idea of what
to do with themselves until the bell went for dinner.

'Sorry to bother you again,' I said cheerily, 'but we need a
bit of help, Dickens and myself, and you look to be just the
men that we need, isn't that right, Dickens?'

'Yes, indeed,' said Dickens from behind me and I was glad

to hear the warmth in his voice. He, like I, had surely noticed the rather forlorn and slightly embarrassed look on the faces of his young visitors and now I saw his eyes sum them up as useful helpers.

Dickens, of course, was famous for putting his guests to work on various projects, most of which were often very much beyond their capabilities. However, it looked as though, this time, that he had struck it lucky. Certainly Swayne, the carpenter was of a different calibre to most of Dickens' friends and there was no doubt in my mind that he would be useful in setting up the stage and the other two brothers looked sturdy and eager to be of assistance as well. I gave them five minutes to settle into the work and then decided that I could melt away.

'My dear Dick,' I said earnestly, 'I have resolved to take your advice. I'm going to write at least a thousand words every day instead of waiting until inspiration strikes. I am profiting from your good example.' I gave a quick wink at Caleb as he, I noticed, looked shocked, but Dickens just laughed and clapped me on the back. He was in a good mood, I noticed. He was a man who loved to give pleasure and he was a born host. The plight of these rather unhappy-looking young men had touched his heart and I could see him determining to make sure that they had an enjoyable Christmas. Even after they had all gone to the schoolroom, I heard him chattering happily to them as they worked.

When, after trying without success to write a page, I abandoned my resolve to work on my latest book, *No Name*, and went to enquire how the stage workers were getting on, I could have patted myself on the back. It had been, I told myself, a clever suggestion of mine to put the brothers at ease by making them part of the workforce.

'Going very well, indeed,' was Dickens' immediate and enthusiastic answer to my quietly spoken question. He did not seem to be doing anything himself, but he beamed approval at Swayne who was directing his brothers.

'I wish that you lived in this country, my friend, and I would employ you to supervise a gang of men and to build a wooden study for me,' he said to Swayne. 'I have an ambition to have a two-storey wooden building with a study on the top floor so that I can get away from everything and concentrate on my book. I own the land across the road, you know, so that would be the place to have it – away from children and dogs and morning callers, not to mention servants asking me what they should do about some problem or being interrupted by a gang of boys going up and down the stairs in hobnail boots.'

I noticed that Swayne was very excited by that prospect. His eyes gleamed, but then a shadow came over them. 'Well, if ever I manage to get the money to set up on my own, I shall certainly get in touch with you, sir,' he said. 'In fact,' he went on enthusiastically, 'I would love to set up a business over here in Kent. Beautiful place and I think that there would be more customers than there are back home where most people are farmers and do their own carpentry. If only I had some money to buy proper tools and set up for myself,' he said, but now I could hear as his voice dropped, that he had little hope of that happening. What a pity, I thought, that this rich aunt had not divided her fortune among these young men, all of whom could have made very good use of it, instead of leaving it to their uncle who, I could not help thinking, may well have already skimmed off the bulk of the money left for the upkeep of his orphaned nephews. Dickens, with his keen understanding of young people, noticed the fall of spirits in the young man's voice and went back to admiring the speed with which his stage was being put together.

'Better than any carpenters have done it before,' said Dickens enthusiastically. 'Well, we'll leave you to it, my friends. Wilkie and I are just a pair of pen pushers – of no practical use at all – come on, Wilkie, let's get out of these hard-working men's way.'

We were just making our way out of the schoolroom when the door was opened by one of the servants.

'Oh, there you are, sir,' she said. 'This gentleman was looking for you and I told him that you'd be bound to be down here getting everything ready for tonight. We're all looking forward to the play very much, sir,' she added and stood back politely to allow Timmy into the room.

He didn't, I thought, look very pleased to see his nephews busily working in the company of Dickens. 'Searching the house for you lot,' he said crisply, 'didn't think to come and tell me where you were, did you?'

Not one of these men was younger than myself, I reckoned, but to my amazement each one of them coloured up and hung their heads like guilty schoolboys. It was embarrassing to watch grown men react like that and I felt quite uncomfortable and inclined to slide out of the room and leave the three of them to their uncle.

Dickens, however, was made of sterner stuff.

'My dear fellow,' he said, taking Uncle Timmy by the elbow and leading him towards the door. 'My very dear fellow, Collins and I were just on the way up to your room to see whether you would join us for a drink and then I have a treat for you. Someone who will be so delighted to meet you.'

Without another word, he steered the man out of the room and towards the library, keeping up a flow of conversation about his visit to Cork and with his usual wonderful memory, producing names and descriptions of the Cork citizens whom he had met in the Imperial Hotel.

'Lovely place to stay in, the Imperial Hotel, in that lovely city of Cork. Best hotel that I've ever known, Collins,' he said without a blush and I who had heard him say the same thing about hotels all over the British Isles suppressed a smile and tried to look impressed. 'What is it that they say in Cork? Yes, I remember it now. "Dublin does it well, but Cork does it better." That was the saying, wasn't it?'

Timothy could not resist this blatant flattery. A pleased smile came over his face and he nodded vigorously. 'Ah, it was a proud day for Cork and for the Imperial Hotel, when they had Charles Dickens staying under its roof,' he said.

Dickens patted him on the back with one hand and with the other opened the door to the library.

'Let's have that drink,' he said and invited his guest to choose from an array of bottles.

'Anything that you are having yourselves,' was the unsatisfactory answer, but Dickens, never a man to stand for these sort of what he called mealy-mouthed manners, poured him a very ordinary whiskey while I helped myself to one of Dickens' exotic liquors from the south of France. I took as long as I could in savouring every mouthful while Dickens, glass in hand, accompanied by his guest, walked the length of his library, reading out the titles of the fake books in his end bookshelf and chuckling over his own cleverness in inventing such pieces of wit as *Views on Emigration*, by the Swallows; *Cats' Lives in Nine Volumes* and *Noah's Arkitecture*.

Timothy, a stupid man, I thought, was so bewildered by these humorous titles, and said so often that he wondered why such a great author did not have multiple copies of his own famous books in his library, that Dickens bored of the sport said decisively, 'Now drink up! There's someone here in Gad's Hill who comes from your own city of Cork, and he will be so excited to meet a fellow Corkonian. Come on, Collins, stop pretending to be a connoisseur and finish up that liquor. I only keep these for the women, you know,' he added impatiently and then turned to his other guest. 'You're finished, are you? Good man, yourself. Let's go!'

Quickly and decisively, he closed the glass door of the bookshelf which held his fake books and walked to the door while Timmy and I obediently choked down the remains of our drinks and followed him. I wondered who this person from Cork was and expected him to lead his guest up to the drawing room, but he didn't. He walked right through the front door, leaving it wide open behind him. I held onto the door handle while Timmy went through and then reluctantly followed my host out into the cold December air, carefully shutting the door behind us, as I could see that Dickens was striding away with great rapidity. Where, on earth, was he going?

Dickens, being Dickens, and always the autocrat, made no explanation, but walked firmly and quickly around the back of the house and headed across the gravel towards the stables. I had a moment's regret that I had not pleaded fatigue or an incipient head cold, as the chilly air struck into my face and penetrated my best suit of clothing. It looked as though horse riding was on the menu. I strongly wished that I were back indoors by one of the roaring fires that Dickens provided for his guests. It was very cold and in addition I, being no equestrian, hoped fervently that we were not going to be forced to ride on one of Dickens' horses to see some beauty spot or to pay a visit to some neighbour's house. The trouble with Dickens was that he threw himself with all the vim of an actor into phases of his own life and now he had tired of being a newspaper man and an editor, he had embarked enthusiastically upon the life of a country gentleman. I fully expected to see three saddled and bridled horses to be led forth, but to my relief only one of the stable hands, wearing an apron and carrying a fork load of soiled straw emerged and looked enquiringly at his master and his master's two guests.

'Well, there you are, Pat, look who I've brought to see you.' Dickens, who was quite an actor, sounded like one who was reuniting boyhood friends and the stable hand looked at him with the wary but slightly amused expression which Dickens' servants, well used to the unexpected, normally wore when suddenly accosted by their master.

Timmy, I noticed, hung back, and taking out a large white handkerchief, spread it over his face in an abortive attempt to blow his nose as Dickens informed his stableman that he had brought him someone that he would be pleased to meet.

I watched with interest. There was some recognition on the stableman's face but no pleasure. Just a slight air of uneasiness – and dislike, I thought.

'Go on, Pat,' said Dickens impatiently. 'Say that rhyme, the one that you were telling me a few weeks ago. Go on! "Are ooo from Cork?" was the first line, wasn't it?'

Pat shrugged with an embarrassed smile. I didn't know how long he had worked for Dickens, but no matter what the length of employment was, he had probably learned that it was the place of a servant to co-operate in keeping one of Dickens' jokes going.

'*Aroo* from Cork?' he said obligingly with an exaggeratedly strong Irish accent, looking invitingly at Timmy who stared blankly at him.

'I am, *aroo*?' said Dickens in a loud whisper into his guest's ear and Timmy smiled in an embarrassed fashion but showed no familiarity with the script. In fact, he was eyeing Dickens' stableman in a wary fashion.

'Go on, Pat,' said Dickens and falling back on me, he said encouragingly, 'You'll enjoy this, Wilkie.'

Pat decided there was no escape and so with a broad smile he said, 'How are the *praaties*?'

'Big and *shmall*,' said Dickens, as always word perfect with his lines.

'Howd'ye *ate* 'em?' said Pat, happily content to pay second fiddle to Dickens' excessively broad Cork accent with as good a version as he could produce after probably spending most of his adult life in southern England.

'*Shkins an-all*!' said Dickens with a flourish and then a roar of laughter as he explained to me that whenever two Irishmen met, even out in places as far flung as New Zealand, they could recognize each other by repeating these lines.

I laughed, too. It really was quite a performance from Dickens and when I noticed the surly expression on Uncle Timmy's face, I laughed even more. Even without the whispered confidences from his nephews, I think I would have disliked this man immensely. He was ignoring Pat as being beneath his attention, keeping his face averted and looking intently at the tree-clad hillside below Gad's Hill Place.

Cork people, Dickens had once told me, are very sociable people and Dickens himself treated his servants as fellow workers so I was not surprised when Pat spoke to Timmy in a friendly fashion.

'What part of Cork do you come from, then? I'd be knowing your face, wouldn't I?'

Timothy looked at Pat rather contemptuously and with a slightly puzzled frown. 'I have a business on North Main Street,' he said.

'Timothy O'Connor is his name,' said Dickens helpfully.

'O . . . h . . .' The monosyllable was dragged out by Pat, and I could see that his face had clouded over. 'I'd better be getting on with my work, Mr Dickens,' he said. He nodded in a friendly way at me – to show that he bore me no ill will about an unfortunate incident in the past when I had dropped the reins of a horse that Dickens was persuading me to mount. The horse had summed me up and had correctly decided that he could do better without me and had instantly galloped off, vaulting the gate, and making for the green hills. It had, I seemed to remember, taken the entire stable staff a good hour to coax him back home again. Pat, I reckoned, would have remembered the incident. I raised an apologetic hand to him; he gave me a forgiving smile, but his fellow Corkonian ignored him and embarked upon a hymn of praise about the view and about the splendour of Dickens' country house and the wonders of the county of Kent.

Pat turned away from him with an unfriendly expression upon his face. The '*Aroo* from Cork?' rhyme or not, it did not appear as if the people of Cork instantly related to each other and so after Dickens had patted his favourite riding horse and given him a lump of sugar, we made our way back to the house with Uncle Timmy leading the way in an assured manner. The day was a fine one and, according to the weather glass in Dickens' hallway, tomorrow was also going to be rain-free.

'I was thinking of us all having a good walk tomorrow morning, get up an appetite for our Christmas Eve dinner. In fact, I was planning on walking over the moors to show you a most interesting church and graveyard near Cooling,' said Dickens and my heart sank. I knew my friend and his walks – thirty miles was nothing to him – the last time that I had visited him he insisted on walking from Folkestone beach to Dover harbour. However, then to my relief, he added, 'But I think we might take Pat and a cart so that any of the women who wish and your little girl and Plorn, perhaps, can ride there and back.'

'Good idea!' I said heartily. I was sure that I could inveigle Carrie into noisily demanding my company on the way home. The trick was to tell her firmly that I was not going to be able to come with her and that would immediately spur her into an assertion that I must and should come in the cart with her and that if I didn't, well, then, she would 'scream and scream'!

In a conscience-stricken way, I now remembered that I had abandoned my charge and resolved to make sure that she was happy, loudly declaring that I must go to see her instantly. Dickens, I had noticed, was tired of Uncle Timmy and his next move would, undoubtedly, be to hand the unpleasant man over to me and request that I entertain him as he, Dickens, busy author that he was, had some work to do before the evening's celebrations. Since I had taken a dislike to Timmy O'Connor, I decided to get out of the way as quickly as I could, so delivered the lame excuse before I could be given the task.

A sudden memory of a neglected child would certainly rank as a plausible excuse in Dickens' mind and so, theatrically, I slapped my hand to my forehead and said, 'Oh my God, I've forgotten about poor little Carrie!' and without waiting for any solution that Dickens might dream up, I took to my heels and literally ran for cover, through the hall door and back up to the library where I could spend a peaceful hour going through Dickens' latest books.

# THREE

D inner, that night, was at an unusually early hour to leave time for the children's play – many of whose actors were of the age when their normal bedtime was eight in the evening.

The food, of course, was wonderful. It always was at Gad's Hill. Dickens, as usual, had made meticulous preparations, but the seating at the table, with four unexpected male guests, had for once upset the arrangements and no name cards were in evidence. People were seating themselves with friends and shortly after most had taken their places I responded to an agonized signal from a friend when Georgina's very large, brown eyes blazed an urgent message to me and then slanted sideways to indicate the right-hand place beside her.

I did not hesitate but went instantly over and slid a leg in front of that chair, just as Uncle Timmy had been about to sit upon it. Already he had a hand upon the back of the chair, but I was a match for him.

'Sorry, old chap,' I said breezily. 'My seat, I think! You kept it for me, didn't you, Georgina?' In a careless, 'old acquaintance' fashion, I leaned over and kissed Georgina's cheek.

'How are you, my dearest girl?' I said in a cordial tone and then as Uncle Timmy, frowning heavily, wandered in a bewildered way to the other side of the room, I whispered in her ear, 'What's the matter? Don't you like the look of him?'

She pursed her lips disdainfully. 'What on earth is Dickens doing, asking a man like that to his house?'

This sounded interesting. So, I was not the only one to dislike 'that man', Uncle Timmy.

'A man like that?' I queried, hitching my chair a little closer to hers and leaning my ear towards her.

O'Connor, I noticed, once cheated of the seat he had intended for his usage, had still not tracked down an empty seat and

was busy seeking a chair among the talkative crowd of Dickens'
guests – few of whom seemed interested in his seatless plight
and many of whom were hastily tilting a chair beside them to
indicate that the seat had been booked.

'Oh, Wilkie, the trouble with you is that you are spoilt,' she
said in an impatient way.

'Spoilt!' I repeated, raising my eyebrows. 'You sound like
my mother,' I added.

'Well, she should know,' retorted Georgina. 'She is the one
who has spoilt you, she, and your father. You've always had
too much money. You just had to ask, didn't you and banknotes
were pushed into your hot little hand.'

'Whereas . . .?' I hinted.

She put her lips to my ear. 'Whereas poor unfortunates like
me get into the hands of moneylenders.' She smoothed the
exquisite silk of her dress which I could have sworn was
made in Paris and said, with a shake of her head, 'And, of
course, you are a man, and you don't care what you wear. A
girl, you know, has to spend money on her clothes. You
wouldn't believe the cost of clothes these days, not like when
you and I were young.' Georgina sighed heavily in a grand-
motherly fashion and then giggled when I told her that I knew
for a fact that she was only nineteen years old and had been
in the schoolroom when she inherited all that money which
had made her the best-dressed lady in London.

'I remember when I was a shy young lad of eighteen years
old,' I said to her, 'and I was seated by a whole cluster of
ladies at a dinner given by the famous Irish painter, Daniel
Maclise.' I pointed across to where Maclise was looking
contemptuously at one of Dickens' favourite Victorian land-
scapes above his fireplace. 'And would you believe me,' I went
on, 'not one of them even smiled at the jokes and *bon mots*
which I had carefully prepared for the occasion. They were
all too busy admiring your dress and wondering whether you
had bought it in Paris.'

She didn't giggle or look pleased, as I had intended, but bit
her lips and shook her head impatiently. 'You see, that's it,'
she said plaintively. 'I got all that lovely money when I was
quite young and so, of course, what was I to do with it, but

cross the sea to Paris and buy gorgeous, expensive clothes. And, you wouldn't understand, Wilkie, but even as a young girl I had perfect taste and soon all London were admiring my dresses. They cost a lot, of course, but I didn't grudge it. What's a girl to spend a fortune on if not her clothes. So, life was wonderful while I had money to buy what I wanted. But now . . . well, what am I to do now?'

I was beginning to understand, though puzzled by the connection to the man whom I had mentally christened as Uncle Timmy. 'And, so,' I said sympathetically, 'if this girl that we are talking about . . . well, if she doesn't have money left over for the new Parisian dress which she has picked out . . .?'

'She has to borrow it, of course,' said Georgina promptly. 'From a moneylender. That's what they are there for.'

'Of course,' I said bowing my head in obedience to that imperious tone. Some men would have been bored with this story, but I had a great love of gossip and never missed the opportunity to hear how my fellow Londoners were managing their affairs. I gave her an encouraging nod and moved my chair just a little nearer to hers.

The table was now sorted out and after a series of swopping of places everyone seemed to have found a seat and Dickens' servants began to serve wine from one end of the table and soup from the other end. Georgina and I were in the centre so had nothing to do but to await their arrival. She put her lips to my ear.

'That new friend of Dickens is a moneylender.'

'Nonsense!' I said, inhaling her perfume. 'He's an Irishman.'

'Yes, of course, he is. I know that! I'm not stupid. I've heard him speak. But a person can be both, can't they? That fellow may be an Irishman, but he is also a moneylender and a most unpleasant man. He even threatened me!'

I thought that she must be joking, but when I turned to stare at her, I saw that her face was white, and her eyes had filled with tears. Whatever the mystery, or whatever the misunderstanding, there was no doubt, but Georgina was in some sort of trouble. I reached out, squeezed her hand, and signalled imperiously at the wine waiter.

'Some wine for the lady,' I said.

He poured a generous glassful and, also, filled my own before going back for another jugful.

'Down the hatch, as they say in the Navy,' I said and squeezed her hand again.

Obediently she drank – quite a liberal mouthful and then leaned across to me. 'I'm not joking, you know. I think that he is the owner of that moneylending firm where I go. He just turns up from time to time, but when he does, everyone, his own staff as well as the customers, seem to be afraid of him. I'm very afraid of him! Oh, Wilkie, what shall I do?'

I gulped down another few mouthfuls of the wine. Not Dickens' best, but it warmed and animated the guests who were all chattering merrily.

'Have another glass,' I said and beckoned again to the friendly wine waiter. I would, I decided, ask no questions. I knew from experience that women confided easily in me and although I was eager to hear the whole story about Uncle Timmy, in my experience, with women, it is best to sit back and allow them to make the pace. Interrogation never worked. I sipped my wine, but did not, however, change the subject.

I gave, I hoped, the impression that I would like to know more if she felt like entrusting me with her story. Why, on earth, I wondered idly, was she going to a moneylender? I had always thought that she was quite an heiress, an only child, both parents dead and she the inheritor of their property and of her grandmother's also, I seemed to remember.

She read my thoughts, I think. However, she waited until her glass was refilled, had one more gulp, then turned to me to continue her story. 'You see, Wilkie, I think that it would have been better if I had not had all that money when I was too young to have sense. I got expensive habits, you see. People expected it of me. They expected to see me dressed in the latest fashions from Paris; they expected my parties to be bigger and better than anyone else; they expected my house to be newly decorated every year; and they expected me to lend them money if they needed it.'

I nodded sympathetically. Most of my friends knew that, until I began to make my own money on my last book, I had barely enough to lead a pleasant life and that I'd had to go to my mother if I needed anything over the normal expenditure. I don't think that anyone would even think of trying to borrow money from me and as for clothes – well I had no interest in them, nor in rich furnishings. Nevertheless, I understood her plight and was sorry for her. I patted her hand and prepared to listen.

'So, you went borrowing money,' I said, to give her a start.

She nodded. 'Yes. In a place in Grafton Street. Someone told me about it. It looked respectable. And the man there seemed so pleasant. Not this man, another man. I signed something, of course. I signed where I was told to, but I was so desperate to get the money that I didn't read it, or didn't understand it properly, but, later, I found that it said that if I didn't pay back by ten o'clock of the morning, three months away, then I would owe them three times the amount. This time it was the unpleasant one, the one that Dickens has invited for Christmas for some reason. But you know how it is, Wilkie. A bill came in from one shop and then from another and I owed my hairdresser quite a sum of money and then my best friend couldn't pay back what she owed me, so I had to go back to these moneylenders and say that I couldn't pay.'

'And they pestered you, I suppose,' I said sympathetically.

'No,' she said, and her eyes opened wide. 'Nobody pestered me. They were very patient, I thought. It was the nice man, again, this time, a man from London and he was very kind, very easy to talk to and most sympathetic, seemed to understand all of my difficulties and he offered me another loan to tide me over until the end of the year when I would have some dividends paid into my bank account – I told him all about my investments and he was very interested and so he drew up another agreement and I suppose that I signed it without reading it properly. I must have, mustn't I? I didn't realize that I had to pay back so much. I just wanted to get out of the mess that I was in.' She stopped there and waited while our plates were filled by the well-trained servant. I said a few words to my other neighbour, enquired about her son who was a budding draughtsman and had drawn an excellent picture of me when he was ten years old. From the corner of my eye, I could see that Georgina was eating nothing, just sitting there with her head bent and stirring her food around the centre of the plate. As soon as I could, I came back to her.

'What are you going to do?' I asked.

She shook her head. She was near to tears.

'He gave me a week to find the money,' she said. 'And if I couldn't, I would have to hand over all my stocks and shares to him. You see, Wilkie, I stupidly . . . well, it seems as though I signed that I would do that. I must have been mad, but I was desperate for money.' She mopped the tears from her eyes and swallowed another mouthful before saying, 'I'll have nothing to live on, then, Wilkie. As a woman, the bank will lend me nothing. I'd never have gone to that moneylender otherwise. I don't know what to do. My solicitor just shrugs his shoulders and suggests that I do the rounds of all my relatives, but I've tried that already and no one is willing to lend me money. Not a farthing. They are all jealous that I inherited so much and all they can say is something stupid and useless like, "You can't possibly have spent all of that money!"'

I could see how that would have been said and how very annoying it must sound to someone in money trouble and so gave a sympathetic nod. Georgina tried to muffle a sob and then said piteously, 'I'll have to go out and scrub floors, or else throw myself into the river. That would be the easiest, I suppose. I don't think that I would be much good at scrubbing floors, but I suppose that even a fool like me can throw herself into the river.'

I was shocked by her words, but my own attempts to find ways for her to earn some money went down badly. To the suggestions that she might become a governess or offer herself as a companion to a rich elderly lady, she kept saying monotonously, 'I'd rather die.'

'Leave it with me,' I said eventually. 'We'll have another talk tomorrow evening. Dickens is planning some Christmas Eve walk or other tomorrow morning and during that I'll really think about your problem, Georgina, and see if I can come up with some solution. Let's not talk about it anymore now. You are just upsetting yourself. Now, excuse me, I must have a word with Jingo about his new boat.'

It was heartless, perhaps, but a good strategy. Jingo Fielding, a nice fellow, but boat-mad, was guaranteed to talk non-stop about his new boat and about all the adventures that he had experienced while sailing from London Steps to Brighton. I leaned across the table and sent a joking question about a report that I had heard about the boat overturning and then the conversation grew general and very animated. Even Georgina forgot her troubles and as Timmy, the moneylender, was at the other end of the long table, she leaned over to chat to the kind-hearted Mrs Dickens, who liked to relate funny anecdotes about her numerous children to a guest who had nobody else to talk to. I checked on her from time to time but decided that she was better forgetting her troubles than going over them again to a man who had no sensible or acceptable suggestions to give her.

I would though, I resolved, without betraying any of Georgina's confidences about her debts, make sure to tell Dickens that one of his guests was an unsavoury moneylender who seemed bent on driving a young girl to a suicidal state. I was sorry for the young men, the nephews, but Dickens might not like to have such an unsavoury type of man as a visitor in his own house. After all, he had his own sons to think of – several of whom were almost grown up, and his daughters, who were, I guessed, not too far distant in years from Georgina. I pondered over this matter as everyone moved into the schoolroom and took their seats in front of the stage.

Before the play began, and as all the cast and crew were preparing for their performance, I made a point of sitting next to Caleb, the literary one of the brothers and, in fact, then moved him away from the rest of his family on the grounds of assisting me as a prompter. Our job – supplying a prompt if a player forgot their lines – was, as usual, superfluous; the cast, as always happened with Dickens' productions, were carefully drilled, but it provided an excuse to keep away from the unpleasant uncle. I decided to strike up another conversation with this young Irish man who was almost the same age as myself. After exchanging a few anecdotes about the unpleasantness of doing work without being interested in it, I approached the subject of his uncle. I had already established such friendly relations with Caleb that he found nothing strange about my interest in his family and he confirmed that his uncle owned a business in London as well as, apparently, a share in a boat that travelled twice a week between Cork and London. A little more probing and I established that the deceased father of the four brothers, together with his young wife, had been a wealthy property owner with a few hundred acres of land on the south-eastern side of Cork city.

'It had been a farm originally,' said Caleb, 'good dry land with a great view of the sea. Well, my father wasn't interested in farming, but he was, I think, a clever man with a good head for business, so he started to sell the land for building, a little at a time. The city started to grow and people with money liked the idea of building houses with sea views and so he decided that he could get better prices for selling the land for building than by selling it to farmers. And so, little by little, he offered small pieces of land to builders – never just one, if I have the story right, he got hold of the names of a few builders who were interested – and then he got them bidding against each other and the prices started to rise. Once some houses were built, well, they were very good houses and so people began to feel that this was a desirable place to live and very soon, so I've heard, there was a new lot of builders queuing up to buy the land. In the end, the whole one hundred acres, left to him by my grandfather, had been sold, and he had a very substantial sum of money in the bank – so a friend of mine who works in the bank, told me once in strict confidence. Swayne was the eldest of the family, but still he was only eight years old when my father and my mother got the cholera. Bypers was a year younger and we, the twins, me and Tiffen, were only five years old. Of course, we were bewildered when we were dressed in black and made to walk behind our parents' coffins. We were too young to understand how our life was changed. Our own lovely house with its big garden overlooking the sea was sold and we were sent off to boarding school, even us two little ones. And when we came home at Christmas we were looked after by a woman, strange to us, who took us into her own house, not the sort of house that we were used to!' Caleb shrugged his shoulders with a look of intense sorrow on his face. 'Suffice it to say,' he said bitterly, 'we longed for the holidays to finish and for the school term to begin.'

I listened with painful interest. What a story of wrongdoing and downright evil. Who on earth could treat four little boys, nephews, sons of his own brother who had died of the cholera – who could treat relatives of his own in such a fashion?

I knew a bit about the price of land for building as my brother-in-law had worked for a property seller at one stage and I could just imagine how Timmy had managed to inherit himself a fortune which would enable him to become an entrepreneur who bought up lucrative businesses, such as a moneylending firm – a dishonest one – and who had proceeded to cheat unfortunates like my poor friend Georgina.

'Have you ever actually seen your father's will,' I asked.

'No, but uncle told us all what was in it,' he said.

A naïve young man, I thought him, but that was the more reason to help him. I gathered my thoughts and endeavoured to give some useful advice.

'Of course, you were too young to understand when your father and mother died, but I'm surprised that you didn't approach the solicitor yourselves when you came of age,' I said. The brothers were all adults, I reckoned. Certainly, they had all left school and had been shoved into jobs, not good jobs, but enough to give them their daily bread and pay for their lodgings, I reckoned. However, no one could say that they were affluent as should have been the sons of a man with a large property that had been sold for building land in a prime part of a rapidly expanding city. I was cautious, though, about advocating action until I knew more.

In the meantime, though, Caleb and I waited for our cue when we had to climb the ladder and sprinkle tiny shreds of white paper to mimic the snow that was falling to cover the stage and set the poor family shivering before their troubles were to be relieved by the arrival of the Ghost of Christmas. The show was about to begin.

Dickens' children had inherited his love of the theatre. And Dickens indulged them hugely in this – always offered help – perhaps too much, I sometimes thought, as the performance

that was laid in front of the guests that night by the children
over seven, would have been impossible for a group of children
if they had not been guided by the genius of their father and
drilled to a degree that was, I always felt, quite unnatural in
children who had all the other excitements of Christmas to
distract them. In fact, Charley, the eldest son, confided in me
that they had planned to do a homemade play with the script
written by Charley himself, the scenery painted by Katy and
the music written by Mamie. However, Dickens had been
determined to put on a professional play for his guests and so
had chosen the play himself and drilled his children meticu-
lously to as near to the standard of professional players as he
could possibly achieve. Neither I nor Caleb had much to do
as prompters and so I watched the audience with interest.

Of course, almost all the light was concentrated upon the
stage, but that was so brilliant that enough was reflected upon
the audience to make the faces visible from the stage and as
I stood idly with the script in my hand, from time to time I
observed a figure moving stealthily through the lines of the
audience, bending down from time to time to whisper in an
ear. I recognized who it was, that was easy enough. It was
the Irishman, the uncle to the four brothers, the man whom
I thought of as Uncle Timmy. But what was he doing? That
was the question. What was he saying? What was he whispering? It appeared to be something of an unpleasant nature.
I looked sideways at Caleb. More conscientious than I,
perhaps, but his eyes were fixed upon the script, and he
appeared to be following, one by one, the words uttered upon
the stage. There was, however, a certain tension about him
as if he were deliberately focusing upon the script and avoiding
looking up from it.

Nevertheless, I was certain in my own mind of the identity
of the moving figure. No mere social chit-chat. These stealthy
visits seemed to cause alarm as heads swivelled and, even
when he moved away, eyes followed him and did not return
to the stage. Even the shouts of laughter and the utterance
of 'bravo!' from the audience appeared to be somewhat
forced.

It was, of course, a singularly silly play, but it was redeemed

by the zest and vigour which the young cast put into it –
Dickens' large family of ten children were actors from a very
early age – and the audience, filled with goodwill after the
excellent dinner and having drunk freely of the wines, gave
them tremendous applause and encores were called for, until
Dickens came onto the stage himself, hoisting young Plorn
high in his arms so that all could see his youngest and then
the audience rose from their seats and shouted their appreciation, until the rafters shook and the young players were taken
off for, in their father's words, a sumptuous feast.

Dickens, I thought, could be a wonderful father on occasion. I remembered hearing that every year all the younger
children were taken to a toy shop a few weeks before
Christmas and allowed to wander all over it while Dickens
feigned to chat with the shopkeeper but kept his ears open
for the shouts of excitement and approval and one of the shop
assistants, supposedly engaged on tidying the shelves, made,
at his request, notes on a piece of paper prepared by Dickens,
where he had listed the names of children young enough to
have a visit from Santa Claus. And then on Christmas morning,
each child got 'surprise' presents that completely fulfilled
their desires!

Dickens would go to any amount of trouble to have a
Christmas which his children would always remember. I sometimes wondered what his own Christmases had been like when
he was a child. Had his boyhood Christmases been perfect,
or had they been for him a disappointment? Dickens, I realized, quite soon after becoming a friend to him, said very little
about his own childhood and I had noticed that his face darkened when questioned upon the subject. I guessed that
Christmas, as he remembered it, may not have been ideal and
so he tried to give his children all that he had been denied
when he was a child. No doubt but that Dickens' ten children
were given an idyllic Christmas.

And now a hugely successful performance, applauded until
the rafters shook, was crowned with a meal that had every
child's favourite food. They had all, each one from eldest to
youngest, been encouraged to request a favourite Christmas
night dish from the cook. The audience was invited to see

them tucking in before we returned to the drawing room to exclaim over the trays of cakes and the decanters of desirable liquors which, during our absence, had been lined up for the delight of the adults in the party.

# FOUR

There was nothing left to chance when you stayed with Dickens for the festival. His Christmas festivals were enormous affairs. Even when, as happened this year, the house was so full that many of the guests had to be boarded out in the Falstaff Inn over the way, or in a nearby cottage, the comfort and entertainment of every single individual guest was carefully catered for. Dickens would, I knew, have taken the whole week off from his work to perfect his plans to entertain his guests. The big mahogany table in the dining room, where we had just dined, had been decorated with vases of red-berried holly, spangled with tinsel. Every picture had sprays of holly tucked behind them and trailing branches of ivy hung from the picture rails, dark green against the white walls and more dangled from the gas brackets. It was a magnificent display, but when we moved into the long drawing room it paled in comparison with that wonderful Christmas scene that now greeted us.

There was a spontaneous outburst of clapping at the splendour of the decorations in the drawing room – not just the holly and ivy, but an enormous pine tree decorated with coloured lamps, silver and gold lengths of tinsel and a multitude of small parcels, all labelled and wrapped in gold, silver and bright scarlet pieces of paper.

Immediately Mamie, Dickens' eldest daughter, moved to the piano and proceeded to thud out a dance tune. Dickens' drawing room was used so often for dancing that he had insisted the carpet was permanently removed and the floor had no covering upon its highly polished wooden boards.

And almost before we could catch a breath, Dickens had everyone dancing. He himself was the most active of all. I had to admire him – a man who was father of ten children, and who was ten years older than myself, born back in 1812, he danced as vigorously as a ten-year-old, clapping his hands to the music and keeping a sharp eye open to make sure that all guests were visibly enjoying themselves upon the well-polished floor of the drawing room. Anyone who quietly slunk away to the side of the room would find that not many minutes had passed before Dickens was jigging up and down energetically, standing right in front of the laggard and summoning him to join in the dance. It was impossible to resist him.

I was probably one of the younger guests, a good ten years younger than most, but I was beginning to flag when Mamie, to my relief, rose from the piano, demonstrating to her father that her fingers ached, by shaking them in his face.

It would have been pleasant at this stage, I thought, if we could have relaxed and chatted among ourselves, but that was not the way things went in the Dickensian household. The evenings before Christmas, as soon as the younger children were sent to bed, were reserved, by tradition, for parlour games, and parlour games had to be played by all. Snap Dragon, Squeak, Piggy, Squeak, Hunt the Slipper and then, of course, Blindman's Buff. As soon as I had said goodnight to Carrie, I prepared to join in with as much gusto as I could muster.

Blindman's Buff was initially rather fun as Dickens, himself, nobly took the part of the 'blindman', allowing his eyes to be bandaged beneath a large scarf, and then stumbled around with lots of near misses and cries of dismay. Dickens, of course, was a born actor, indeed, he has often told me that, but for the bad luck of having a severe cold in the head on the day when he was to be interviewed for what would have been his first part as an actor, he would have made a career on the stage, instead of becoming known as a writer. Certainly, his performance as the blindman was a masterpiece of feigned stumbles, cries for pity and shrieks of triumph when he captured the sleeve of some daring guest and dismal howls of despair when the victim managed to escape or was incorrectly named. I do believe that he was enjoying this so much that he would have gone on for a large part of the evening if I had not clumsily stumbled over the protruding leg of a spindly seat and literally fallen into his arms.

'A catch, a catch!' he yelled theatrically. His hand went

swiftly to my face and plucked my spectacles from above my nose.

'The man in specs, himself!' he declared, to be greeted with a howl of laughter. 'It has to be Wilkie! What do you say, ladies and gentlemen, is it Mr Wilkie Collins?'

'Easy to guess,' said Hablot Knight Browne, an illustrator friend of Dickens' and not a man I liked too much. 'A tiny little man wearing glasses. Has to be Wilkie!'

It was, I thought, as I accepted the blindman's scarf, a rather unnecessarily spiteful observation, but I forced a smile upon my face and allowed myself to be turned three times by Dickens, before setting off to walk around the room with the traditional groping movements of the blindman. I had thought that it might be rather fun to do as Dickens had done and to mime the performance of an actor. In fact, during his performance I had almost wished to be the centre of attention just as he had been. Certainly, he had filled the room with shouts of laughter and the atmosphere had been full of enjoyment.

However, after he caught me and I had taken on the role of blindman I didn't find it so entertaining and once I had tripped over an easy chair for the second time, I tore off my bandage and proposed that we would have a change of game. Others also had tired of the dodging around the room and agreed happily to the suggestion from Uncle Timmy that they play a favourite from Christmas celebrations in his native country of Ireland. It was, he told us with the air of presenting something new and strange, called the Memory Game. We all knew it, of course. A game from most people's childhoods where each player having successfully enumerated the previous sentence adds a new phrase to those that went before. At least all could sit on comfortable chairs, drink liqueurs and eat slices of Christmas cake while playing the game with as much attention as suited our individual natures. The only difference between the game as we played it and the game as they played it in Ireland was that, apparently, in Ireland, the phrases had to be nothing but addresses, either real, or made up.

'Gad's Hill,' I declaimed when the spinning of the wheel pointed to me as the first to utter an address. A good idea, these addresses, I thought, and then sat back. I hoped others would follow my example and say something memorable. Real addresses would make it easy for everyone to be reasonably successful – and would keep the game going for the desirable amount of time. As I hoped, most of the addresses which tripped out from every player were either familiar or easily memorized.

But, of course, Dickens had to come up with something unexpected – not any of his own addresses and certainly not a well-known place.

'Warren's Blacking Factory, thirty The Strand,' he declaimed and, oddly, I saw O'Connor give him a sharp look, and scribble something in a notebook which he took from an inner breast pocket of his jacket. There was, I thought, some mystery about this place.

When it came to Uncle Timmy himself, the man did not hesitate, just reeled off the list and then added his own contribution. 'Number forty-five, Grafton Street,' he said, and an odd silence came over the noisy, chattering crowd, and I wondered whether this was the place which Georgina had mentioned. A few nervously swallowed a drink, while others looked around the room with feigned expressions of indifference. There were some to whom the address meant nothing, but a surprising amount of the guests reacted to it. Georgina, I noticed, looked quite terrified. There was no doubt in my mind that this address: forty-five Grafton Street was the address of the moneylender's premises. And no doubt, also, that Georgina was not the only person in the room to have got themselves into the hands of an unscrupulous usurer. Uncle Timmy had not only been the one to propose this game, but he had unexpectantly taken charge of the room and arranged the chairs in a circle so now, I noticed, he was able to keep an eye on all faces.

'Your turn again, Dick,' I said as I could see that even our host was distracted by the uneasy atmosphere that had interrupted his carefully planned evening of laughter and merriment.

Dickens paused for a moment. There was, I noticed, an odd expression upon his face. He looked around at the guests and then said, quite rapidly, and almost without thinking repeated, 'Warren's Blacking Factory, number thirty The

Strand.' And then he looked around the room with an odd expression which seemed to challenge all to comment. It might have been my imagination, but I thought that there was something strange about the emphasis that he put upon what must surely have been some random address that had taken his fancy when he was walking through London. My eye was caught by the sight of Uncle Timmy fixing a strange gaze upon his host and Dickens stared back at him defiantly, while waiting for the next in line to attempt to enumerate all. Nevertheless, as Walter, Dickens' second eldest son, failed miserably to recite the list, I noticed that Uncle Timmy had once again slipped a notebook from his pocket and was scribbling something upon one of the pages. Was it, I wondered, that strange address given by Dickens, that had taken his attention? Or another address, the name of what sounded like a stately home in Kent, mentioned by young Edward Thompson. It was that one, I thought.

Edward Thompson was a young man of good family. He had probably been in school in France with one of Dickens' sons. I guessed that the address given had been that of his parents' or grandparents' home. The name of a village in Kent, finished off with the word 'House' sounded to me like one of those big, expensive dwelling places.

I tightened my lips. The moneylender had scribbled something, the address doubtless, upon a notebook taken from the breast pocket of his suit and there was no doubt in my mind that this unpleasant man would tackle the parents, or grandparents, if young Ted Thompson had borrowed money and was unable to keep up with his payments. The uneasy glances that the young Ted sent in Uncle Timmy's direction made me sure that he was in the moneylender's hands. Tired of the game and worried by the tense faces, I made a mistake and dropped out of the five who were left in the contest. I wished that the evening was over and that we were all allowed to seek our beds and that those worried by the presence of a moneylender would be able to get a good night's rest. I was just about to suggest a brandy for everyone, followed by an early bedtime, when Dickens forestalled me.

'Dumb Crambo,' he shouted, and I nodded happily. Dickens

was the consummate host and had picked up on the atmosphere. And he knew that now was not the moment for bed when the guests were uneasy and slightly troubled.

I was happy to play Dumb Crambo and immediately volunteered to be a team leader. Quite a fun game, a game in which one team chooses a word to be guessed and gives a rhyming word as a clue to the other team which then pantomimes its guess as to the original word. Households all over London and Kent would be playing that game on this night before Christmas.

'Dumb Crambo, my favourite game,' said Jas Morehouse, quick to pick up the atmosphere. So far, he had stayed out of the more energetic of the games, demonstrating a bandaged wrist as his excuse, but now he showed his enthusiasm by clapping silently. Jas was one of my favourite of Dickens' friends. Older than Dickens and older than most of his friends, he was, I always thought, one of the nicest of men, a widower with a tragic history of losing his wife and fifteen-month-old twin sons twenty years ago and with the reputation of staying completely faithful to her memory and to the memory of his young boys since then. Jas was no farmer, but he owned large estates of apple orchards that supplied the London markets with high quality eating apples. He was immensely well off and the soul of generosity as was well known to every charity and to his young relatives. I knew him through Dickens, because they had both been involved in a charity that had provided shelter and a hot meal for women of the night, on cold and wet weather. He was, I found, always interested in his fellow men, anxious to hear about any successes, whether small or large and ready to console and to advise whenever life was not going well for one of his numerous friends and acquaintances. He was the first that I picked for my team, and characteristically he was the one who had hit upon a word with plenty of opportunities for comic miming, so that we could all set to work with enthusiasm to devise a sketch which would be fair to our opponents but would hopefully defeat their endeavours to guess our word. We had just huddled together, all with frowning brows, thinking hard, when Jas came up with the word 'dead'.

'Too easy,' said John Forster, one of Dickens' oldest friends.

'But think of all the rhyming words,' I said hastily. As group leader I was determined to discourage any non-constructive criticism. It had the effect of dampening creativity; I had always found.

'True,' said Maclise. 'Head. Said. Bread. I can think of dozens more.'

'The mime will have to be complicated since the word is so easy.' John Forster was determined to be negative. 'How can you mime the word "dead"?'

Jas shrugged his shoulders. 'Easy,' he said. 'You are lucky enough to have Arthur Sullivan, the musician, here tonight, he is a friend of Dickens' son Charley, isn't he? Can't beat his voice, can you? He can stay behind the door and sing "Abide with Me". Someone will be the corpse and we'll all stand around and pretend to sing.'

And so, Arthur Sullivan stood behind the door and sang the hymn, while Jas, himself, lay across three chairs, covered by a white sheet purloined by Dickens' daughter Katy from the linen cupboard and the rest of us stood around the body with the solemn faces of mourning friends and relations and the few musical guests sang softly in accompaniment to the lovely voice of Arthur Sullivan. Apart from the muted singing, the rest of the acting was in dumb show as we hung our heads and mopped our eyes with a great flourish of hand-kerchiefs and Jas, with his very colourless face made, I thought, an excellent corpse as he lay motionless across the three chairs, and the rest of us did our best. I could hear the mutters from the audience as we played the part of grieving relatives and I thought that most seemed to be led astray by the funeral pageant.

The shouts from the audience came fast as soon as we relaxed and turned, with broad grins, to receive their guesses. Oddly the word 'dead' did not come up. I had a strong suspicion that by this stage in the evening most of the guests had already imbibed a little too much alcohol and that their host was only too delighted to sense a convivial atmosphere to worry about the solving of a puzzle or the winning of a game. A Christmas atmosphere was what my friend wanted and that was what had emerged. Perhaps led by Dickens who instantly shouted 'corpse', words like 'burial', 'funeral', 'graveyard', 'church' were abundant. Few seemed to go back to the 'sounds like' examples that we had given and none of the words shouted came near to our original hint of 'sounds like head'. In the end, prompted by Dickens, they gave in amid shouts of laughter and asked for the solution.

'One mark to my team,' I shouted joyfully and we all shook hands with each other before changing places and sitting down on the chairs, prepared to demolish Dickens' team who had chosen a word.

'Sounds like "host"' announced his spokesperson and my team amused themselves with shouting words like 'toast' and 'roast'. The fourth round of drinks had been handed around and it seemed to me that my team were not using their brains. Some were openly drunk, signalling at Dickens' man to refill their glasses, and others, as I saw when I looked back over the rows, were exchanging jokes, or like Georgina seemed to be absorbed in a private conversation with Jas. Telling him her troubles, I guessed, feeling quite annoyed with Georgina. The man looked most unwell and should not be asked to bear another's problems. Poor fellow, there was an expression of grave concern upon his face and already Georgina had produced one of her lace-edged handkerchiefs and was daintily mopping her eyes. Jas was such a nice man. Earlier on I had noticed him listening, with that very same expression, to his own young nephew, George Symonds. As soon as he had finished listening to Georgina, he went across to refill her glass of wine and she appeared to cheer up very much as soon as she drank from it.

# FIVE

I went off to bed with the strong resolution to be of assistance. I told myself that although I could not solve these
money problems of my poor friend, Georgina, I would do
my best to make sure that she had a happy Christmas and
when I met her over Christmas Eve breakfast the following
morning, I determined to make sure that she did not stay in
her bedroom worrying about the year to come, but that I would
induce her to join the party on one of Dickens' favourite walks
from Gad's Hill, through the village of Higham and across to
Cooling church where he promised to show us the most
intriguing grave that we had ever seen – so intriguing, in fact,
that he proposed to have it form the backdrop to his latest
novel. Those who came, would, he promised them, be in at
the birth of the best book which he had ever produced and
that was a bribe which few could resist. In the end, quite a
number eagerly agreed to join in the walk and assist in the
production of yet another worldwide bestseller.

As usual with Dickens, a born organizer, everything was
arranged by his staff and family as quickly as possible. Pat
was coming with the wagon to carry the packed lunch and to
transport any young child whose legs began to get weary, or
any delicate female who became too tired to walk home. Two
of Dickens' older sons would be on hand to help with organizing the picnic lunch and everything would be done for the
enjoyment of his guests.

The day was a perfect one for a walk and we set off under
a blue sky in bright winter-time sunshine and all were in high
spirits, singing loudly. The children, were, in the end, just little
Carrie and her new best friend, seven-year-old Plorn, as
Dickens' youngest son was nicknamed. They would soon tire,
I thought, but it was good for Carrie to have a companion of
a similar age and I liked to watch the pair of them trying to
outdo each other in singing 'Jingle Bells'.

It was all well planned. The cart picked up the children and
a few of the ladies when we came within a mile or so of
Cooling church, but for the rest of us the sudden appearance
of the church spire and of the ship's beacon in the distance
was enough to encourage our failing energies.

'I see the sea!' sang Carrie, standing up very straight and
holding onto the collar of Pat's jacket.

'It's not the sea; it's the estuary of the River Medway!'
called Frank, one of Dickens' older sons, but Carrie, who was
used to being told she was right, drowned out his voice with
the chant of, 'I see the sea and the sea sees me.'

'I see ships,' shouted Plorn. 'Big, big ships.'

'Hulks,' contradicted Frank. 'They're prison ships. Convicts
on them.'

'What's convicts?' said Carrie and I was proud of her. She
was only five years old, but already she had a great interest
in words.

'Bad men – they are very bad men – they eat little girls,'
called out Timmy and I looked at him with dislike. Carrie's
face looked troubled. She and her mother had been almost a
year with me now and I think she had grown into a happy
and very secure little girl, liked by all my friends and, of
course, indulged by me. Nevertheless, she was too young for
sour comments like that. I opened my mouth to try to explain
to her that it was just a joke, but I was forestalled by another
child.

'They don't,' said Plorn, scornfully. 'That's silly nonsense.
No one eats little girls or little boys, either. Anyway, my father
says that some convicts are good men, but that they did something bad like stealing because their family was hungry. And
he knows more about convicts than you do. So there,' added
this fearless son of a radical writer and I was delighted to see
how the moneylender scowled while Dickens laughed.

He was, however, a good host and explained to all that the
convicts were doing great work in widening and deepening
the river and building up the marsh land with the spoil which
they took from the bed of the estuary. I watched the poor
fellows with pity, many of them up to the tops of their legs
in the river water filling buckets with yellowish clay soil and

attaching the buckets to the wires in a pulley that brought the buckets to a place at the top of the cliff where they could be emptied on to the marsh.

'Great work,' repeated Dickens. 'Serves the community. They are widening and deepening the river before it enters the sea, and they are building up the land so that the church and the houses don't get flooded by the river.'

'Poor things,' said Georgina pityingly and Carrie immediately echoed her words and looked sorrowfully at a convict who had just slipped and fallen, emptying the bucket full of yellow sodden earth back into the estuary again. The overseer cracked a whip once across the man's shoulders, but upon seeing the crowd of ladies and gentlemen looking down on him, he moved away and started to shout at another group of convicts.

'Let's get out of here,' I muttered to Dickens as I saw Carrie's eyes widen with horror and noted how Plorn stuck his thumb into his mouth. Dickens patted his little son on the back and, of course, he rose to the occasion.

'There's the church that I was telling you about,' he called, pointing to the steeple and adding, 'We'll have our picnic there, Plorn, won't we. It's nice high ground and we have brought some rugs to sit upon.'

I averted my eyes from the unfortunate men in the river and concentrated on admiring the church. Convict ships were a necessity, I supposed. The prisons were full up because of the unrest caused by the lack of jobs, the lack of food and the lack of housing. No friend of a radical writer like Dickens could be left in ignorance about the conditions suffered by the poor of a country which should have enough money for all of its citizens.

'Let's get to the church,' I called out with feigned eagerness. I began to wish that Dickens had not brought us to this desolate spot. It was marsh country with an unhealthy feel to the air. It was, I thought, a bleak place, overgrown with nettles, even in the churchyard. Beyond the churchyard there was nothing but wilderness, intersected with dikes and mounds and gates and here and there with scattered cattle feeding on the rank grass from the marshes. The sea was in the distance, I knew, but there was no invigorating salt in the air – just a dank, ugly place with a smell of decay. What the cattle found to eat, I knew not, as all that I could see were rushes, rank marsh growth in between the alder trees and pollards.

'Up this path,' said Dickens cheerfully and we followed him obediently. I kept near to the cart as I could see that little Carrie's face still looked downcast and I began to fabricate a happy ending for one of those convicts that she looked at so pityingly. He would, I told her, find a pot of gold, and go back to his family and buy them a wonderful meal of roast chicken. And they would live happily ever after. All of Carrie's stories had to end with these magical words. Her recollections of her early life when she wandered the streets with her mother were still there, I reckoned, from time to time – deeply buried, not to be talked about, but ready to come to the surface when any unusual or distressing event caused the confident little girl to retreat into a shell and observe the world around her with wide, distressed eyes.

'This way, everybody,' shouted Dickens and I obediently followed, though I kept one hand on the cart as we went up a small hill towards Cooling church.

'Come on, Plorn, give us a song,' shouted Dickens and Plorn immediately lifted his head and sang in his high, pure voice 'Miller and His Men' that Dickens loved, a song that dated from his own childhood. As soon as I heard Carrie's voice join in with the chorus, 'When the wind blows, the mill goes', I took my hand from the back of the cart and slowed my footsteps. That evil man, Timmy, that moneylender who threat-ened women and robbed children of their innocent belief in the goodness of the world around them, was at his old tricks, walking beside Swayne and, from what I could see, hissing in the young man's ear. Then they both stopped. Swayne looked distressed, I thought, as I lingered for a moment, pretending to examine the convict ship out on the water, with one hand to shield my eyes and then moving my head so that I could see the two figures standing in the road, facing each other. With his bulk and height, Swayne was twice the man that his uncle was, but he hung his head, like a boy who has been whipped, and scuffed the dust on the little road with one foot. And then I saw Timmy take his hand from his pocket and hold it out, palm upwards, with an imperious gesture. There was a moment when neither moved but both seemed to eye each other in a silent battle.

There had to be a winner, of course. And, now that I knew the history of this man and his nephews, I was not surprised when the tall, burly carpenter, a man who worked with his hands and who probably had the strength to toss the older man into the ditch, put one large hand into his trouser pocket, extracted a purse, took a coin from inside it and handed it over to his uncle. I saw it flash and realized that it was a gold coin. And then Swayne, with the air of one who distances himself from evil, strode up the hill with such speed that the older man was left behind. Uncle Timmy didn't appear to mind though, and his attention was focused on the coin in his hand. He lifted it to his mouth, bit it and then, with an air of satisfaction, placed it within his own purse and stood back and waited in the centre of the road for the cart with the two singing children to catch up with him.

Dickens was just behind me, chatting with his great friend, Maclise, but I interrupted an anecdote and called out impera-tively, 'Dick, don't let that man into the cart with these two children!'

I saw surprised looks on both faces and fumbled for an explanation which would be convincing, but would not betray my instinctive dislike and abhorrence of that man.

'It's not fair,' I said, trying to make a joke out of it. 'If one man goes in the cart, then all the rest of us must be allowed to crowd into it. No discrimination, Dick. That's our watch-word, isn't it?'

Dickens gave me a piercing look of interrogation, but he did not hesitate. He never did. I've seldom met anyone whose mind worked so quickly and who rarely took more than a couple of seconds to come to a decision.

'No discrimination! No men in the cart, only children and perhaps some very tired ladies,' he boomed in a voice that would have carried to the other end of the marshes.

Timmy turned his head to look down the road while Pat

shook the reins and urged the horse to a quicker step. I was glad that I had intervened. I had done it for my little Carrie's sake, but now that I was a little nearer to the cart, I could see that the back seat was loaded with picnic baskets and the seat beside the driver was occupied by the two small children. There, genuinely, was no room for another passenger on this outward journey. I smiled to myself and waited for Dickens and his companion to catch me up. I would stay with them, I decided. If I didn't, then this obnoxious Timmy would probably force his company upon me.

'Magnificent place, Dick! What an excellent choice for a winter walk' I said. Dickens, I knew, loved to have his judgement praised and to be able to display his knowledge of the countryside where he had, after all his years as a Londoner, now made his home. 'Why are there so many little hillocks on the marsh?' I asked and was not surprised when he proved to be full of information.

'Well, you see before you, my friends, a good example of allowing the sinner to make payment to society for his crimes. These men that you see with their buckets and their spades are doing two services to those of us who use our mighty River Medway and those of us that love the land around it,' he said, including us all in his explanation. 'Every bucket of earth and slime that is dug out from beneath the shallow edge of the river is deposited upon the marsh. Before this work began, the marsh was waste land, nothing but puddles and a few coarse rushes, useless to man and beast, but now look at it. Look at those cows! See how they feed upon that good juicy grass that is beginning to grow on those clumps from the bed of the river.'

Dickens, I thought, had a gift; a gift that did not just make him a brilliant writer, but a great speaker as he had a way with words, which even in a casual conversation, would open a person's eyes to something which otherwise he would pass by without a second glance. As he instructed me on the valuable work being done by the convicts in reclaiming the land, I could see a strange beauty in the marshes, the clumps of green, the black horizontal line of the river, the gleams of white from sea-scoured and rain-washed stones that had been placed here and there, probably for stepping-places when the rains were heavy, or for use when the tide was in. From his words, I could see that there might be a possibility that these men, looking every day at what their labour had achieved, might be led to a better way of life. I hoped so, indeed, and shared his view that this was a better and a more humane way of dealing with convicts, rather than just locking them up and depriving them of human company or the possibility of doing good.

# SIX

The lane leading to the churchyard was very steep and so to save the already tired horse, Dickens and I removed the two children from the cart and allowed them to scamper ahead of us up to the church where, as Dickens promised his weary guests, a sumptuous lunch would be eaten.

Carrie and Plorn, fresh as daisies after their ride in the cart, began to run towards the church, while I paused and waited for my friend Georgina, who was looking exhausted.

'Why does he always have to inflict this upon his guests,' she said in a savage undertone. 'Just because he likes to go on thirty-mile walks it doesn't mean that the rest of us enjoy it!'

'Never mind,' I said consolingly as I offered her my arm. 'There's a magnificent lunch in those baskets at the back of the cart and as for wine . . . well, I could hardly count the number of bottles which are stored beneath the seats.'

She took my proffered arm and even smiled a little. There was no doubt in the mind of any of Dickens' guests that, no matter what feats of athleticism and endurance he would impose upon them, the food and the drink was invariably of the highest quality. That made up for a lot, was the opinion of most of his guests.

We had struggled almost halfway up the narrow lane to the little church and the two children, full of energy after their long ride, had gone well ahead of us, wanting to be the first to reach the churchyard, when there came a scream from Carrie which made my blood run cold. My first instinct was to look back and assure myself that the villain, Timmy, was nowhere near to them, but I was reassured. No, he was walking along and talking with Daniel Maclise. Nevertheless, I dropped Georgina's arm and began to run up the hill and Dickens, who was always on the alert, joined me in under a minute.

Neither of us spoke. The scream had not been repeated,

but that was, I feared, even more alarming. We went at a speed that made little of the steepness of the narrow little road and then as we came through the gate the sound of high, excited voices relieved our anxiety. I slowed to a walk, putting a hand to the painful stitch in my right side, but Dickens, the father of eight lively sons, who was more used to running than I, was through the churchyard gate while I still struggled up the steep hill.

'What's the matter, Plorn?' I heard him shout. I could not make out the answer, but two cheerful and excited voices were competing with explanations and the thud in my heart slowed down as I changed from a frantic run to a sedate scaling of the slope. He had left the gate open behind him, so I was not long in coming through into the churchyard and was immensely relieved to see a little figure in a bright red coat.

'It's ghosts,' shouted Carrie as I came into sight. 'Ghosts made from stone. It is really, really scary!'

There was no sign of Dickens or of little Plorn, but my Carrie was there, safe and sound.

'Oh, Carrie,' I said reproachfully. 'You gave me a fright.'

'I got a worser fright than you!' Carrie could never endure to be found in the wrong and it was always useless to argue with her.

'What gave you the fright?' I enquired, trying to suppress an indulgent smile.

She came up close to me, her eyes as wide as saucers, her mouth slightly open as she strove for the best effect.

'Ghosts,' she breathed. 'Ghosts, but a good magician has turned them to stone so they can't hurt you.' Nevertheless, she slipped her little hand into mine and I held it firmly.

'Show me,' I said.

'Let's run,' she said, and I knew that she was no longer frightened but resolute to milk the experience to its last drop and unwilling to allow Plorn to claim to be the owner of the ghosts.

'There they are!' she said triumphantly as we came through the bramble-covered churchyard where the dwellers of the little village nearby were laid to rest once their earthly days were over.

And then I saw what had frightened the two young children.

On top of one of the graves there were twelve stone lozenges, each carved in the shape of a small child, each about a couple of feet long, and all arranged in a neat row. The heads were carved into a rounded shape, but the face was eyeless and mouthless which added to the ghostly impression. I felt Carrie's little hand squeeze mine and I picked her up and held her tightly in my arms.

'Wonderful, aren't they?' said Dickens. 'Just something about them that inspires me. One day I will compose a book about this place. What an atmosphere, eh!' He looked down at his small son. 'You see, Plorn, the family wanted to remember their children who died when they were young, so they got a stonemason to make little statues, little dolls of them,' he said. 'That was a good idea, wasn't it?'

Plorn nodded, but rather doubtfully and Carrie bit her lip.

I was beginning to wish that we had never come to this place. It was not good for two small children like Carrie and Plorn to hear of the death of children.

'Why did they die?' asked Plorn. He had a frightened note in his voice, and I remembered, suddenly, that one of his little sisters, Dora, had died in infancy.

'Marsh ague,' said Dickens cheerfully.

'Marsh ague,' said Plorn to Carrie.

Carrie then repeated, 'Oh, marsh ague!' in a dubious-sounding tone of voice.

She had an unhappy, worried look about her.

'It was a long, long time ago,' I said hastily. 'You will not get it. And Plorn will not get it. We have no marshes where you live and, anyway, nowadays, doctors are clever and they can make children better. Do you remember the nice red medicine that you got from the kind doctor? And it made you stop coughing? You really liked that medicine, Carrie, didn't you?'

Carrie said nothing for a minute but then she struggled from my arms and went over to the grave. Plorn dropped his father's hand and went to join her.

'I'd like to take them home,' she said. 'I could make a bed

for them in my room. They must be cold out here. They will get a cough if they catch cold in this place.'

'They're not here,' said Dickens decisively. 'These are just models of children, just like you and Plorn make with clay. Just pretend – just like dolls. But someone owns them so you cannot take them. That would be stealing. You know the ten commandments, Plorn. Say them for Carrie.'

And Plorn obediently began to recite, 'First I am the Lord thy God . . .' He continued solemnly and when he arrived at: 'Eight: thou shalt not steal,' Dickens stopped him.

'You see, Carrie, you must not steal. God tells us that.'

There was something about Dickens, some strong inner belief in himself, that invariably convinced both adults and children that he knew what he was talking about. Carrie nodded obediently and I looked around the graveyard to see if I could direct her attention to something else.

But by now, to my intense relief, the rest of the party started to stream in through the churchyard gate. Plorn and Carrie competed as to who could tell them first about the stone children and it turned into a competition between the two children as to who remembered the most about marsh ague and the word stonemasons and it was an opportunity for some excited showing off on the part of the children as the grown-ups made noises of astonishment and pity.

Timmy, elbowing one of his nephews aside, came to the forefront of the group and bent down. 'Wonder how heavy it is,' he said. Bending down he picked up one of the small figures with an ease that showed the man was quite strong. He glanced around for admiration while holding the small figure aloft but there was a low murmur of disapproval and most turned away from him and looked around the graveyard.

'Not here for the picnic. Certainly not!' said someone and there was a murmur of agreement.

'Really?' queried Dickens, but I who knew him well, recognized a note of relief in his voice. He may have planned for the picnic to take place in this interesting spot, but Dickens was an artist. The starkly pitiful sight of the little effigies would, I was sure, prove an inspiration to him for a new book, but the sad atmosphere might be spoiled by the memory of cheerful and merry voices as they ate from plates and dishes placed on the stones or even on top of these pathetic figures. I looked around at the dark flat wilderness beyond the church-yard. It was, I could see, dotted with dykes that in those winter months had been filled with rainwater. There were also various mounds and attempts at making corrals for the cattle by circular banks furnished with rusty gates and then, in one place, at the top of the hill, was a semi-circle of alder trees – bare of leaves now in this month of December but the alder was a tree, I seemed to remember, that needed damp condi-tions and would suck in the water from the soil around its roots. The earth beneath, and in front of them, would have been sucked dry during the summer months and I could see that there were several storm-felled trees which could provide seating for the guests. I moved a little closer to Georgina.

'What about up there?' I murmured in her ear with a nod in the direction of the trees. 'Under the alder trees up there?' I indicated them but spoke in a low voice and she immediately picked up on the suggestion, going straight over to Dickens.

It worked well. Dickens liked to be in charge, and I was fairly certain that he had originally planned the rather macabre setting of the grave with its stone effigies as an amusing setting for an unusual picnic. He would, I thought, have been happy to overlook the fact that his own small son was unlikely to share the joke. But I was, certainly, not going to expose Carrie to something which might give her nightmares for years. The setting on the top of the hill, under these alder trees would make a lovely place for a picnic, sitting on some felled tree trunks and gazing towards the estuary of the River Medway where the waves crashed against the rocks. He would brush aside my protests, but he was very chivalrous and loved to please his lady guests. Georgina was the woman to convince him of that. I waited until his head nodded approval and then diverted him.

'What's that, Dick?' I shouted across to him. I pointed at a tall structure made from pieces of metal that stood high upon a bank beside the river, just near to where the convict ships were moored. It had something like an unhooped cask upon the pole – an ugly thing. I could not imagine what it could be used for.

That distracted him. He loved to inform.

'It's a beacon,' he called back. 'The men on the prison ships maintain it. It guides the ships coming into Rochester or London harbour. They hang lanterns on it at night and when the fog is dense to direct the ships to harbour. And, look over there, look at that other piece of metal. Fifty years ago, that would have held a pirate some time, he'd be hung up there on chains and left until the end came for him.'

A terrible death, I thought with a shudder and was glad that these days such a terrible drawn-out death was no longer imposed upon criminals such as pirates. I looked hastily around but the two young children were running races on the slope from the church door to the gate and they had taken no notice of my query. They looked busy and happy and so I was able to help with setting up the lunch. After the distance that all had walked, keeping to Dickens' brisk pace, most of the guests were probably looking forward to rest and some tasteful food.

Georgina had instantly convinced Dickens that the dry ground under the alder trees would be ideal for the picnic and already he was gathering some helpers to aid Pat in carrying the hampers from the cart. Uncle Timmy, I noticed, was bringing a case load of wine and I hoped that he would not drop it. I stayed where I was. It had, after all, been my discovery and I had already worked out where the rugs were to be placed so that an unobstructed view could be had of the turbulent waters where the River Medway encountered the salt waters of the ocean. I busied myself by collecting some sawn sections of tree trunk for those who did not want to sit upon the ground. By the time that Pat, carrying the rugs by the simple method of draping them around his shoulders, arrived with a box of wine, I was ready to issue some directions.

'Make sure that fellow doesn't go off with the drink,' hissed Pat, moving a thumb in the direction of Uncle Timmy and then parking the box of wine bottles on top of a large flat stone in a place where it would be conspicuous to all.

'And him a fellow Irishman,' I said in an undertone. 'I thought that the two of you would be best of friends. You don't think that an Irishman would steal the wine, do you? Isn't Ireland supposed to be the island of saints,' I added, and he gave me a sour grin.

'Don't know who told you that piece of nonsense,' he said. 'Plenty of scallywags in Ireland,' he added and waited with his box until Dickens himself arrived.

Pat, I noticed, relaxed visibly, once his master was on the scene and he allowed Dickens to throw out orders to some of the strongest-looking male guests and soon there was a line of people coming from the cart, weighed down with boxes and hampers and when all of these had been brought over, a large sack stuffed with cushions arrived. Dickens handed this sack over to me with the instruction: 'ladies first' and I walked around with my welcome gifts of these so very well-stuffed cushions while Dickens chose two of his older sons, Walter and Frank, to bring around the drinking glasses and he himself followed with the wine. Pat and I were then delegated to serve the sandwiches. John Forster was put in charge of slicing the magnificent cake, which was sent every Christmas to the Dickens household by Angela Burdett Coutts, heiress to the Coutts Bank fortune who was godmother to his eldest son, Charley. Dickens did a lot to help the wealthy heiress spend her money on suitable charities and the annual Christmas cake was one of the ways in which she endeavoured to thank such a busy man, even to the extent, once, of sending the awe-inspiring cake across Europe on one Christmas when the Dickens family spent the holiday in Italy.

I still remember the pleasantness of that lunch. The weather, so cold the night before, had suddenly become warmer, mellow sunshine and nothing but the slightest breeze. From where we sat, eating and drinking, we no longer had sight of the prison ships, nor of the unfortunate convicts toiling in the mud and sending bucket after bucket of that yellow, almost liquid, slimy earth, dug up from under the water, along the shoreline and then up the cliff to be emptied upon the marsh. No such unpleasant sights from our well-chosen picnic place. The two children, my own little Carrie, and Dickens' youngest son, Plorn, sat with me, and I was glad to see that they had forgotten all about those pathetic stone figures and the sad story of so many children from the one family dying in their youth from the ague – a form of malaria, I guessed, and wondered why the family had not moved away to a healthier environment. I shuddered at the thought of losing all those children at such an early age and then distracted myself by teaching Carrie and Plorn a few sentences in French so that if the sailors from the French ship came ashore, we could ask them how they were and offer them a slice of cake.

It was while we were wondering where the ship might land and trying to choose a good place for it to come ashore and while the two children, now tired of eating, were busy peering expectantly over the nearby wall that I noticed that man, whom I still thought of as 'Uncle Timmy', surreptitiously filling one pocket with a parcel of sandwiches and sliding a bottle of wine into the opposite pocket of his brightly coloured sou'wester, which frankly looked rather odd out here on the marshes. He stood for a few minutes talking to one of Dickens' friends, then moved away, standing for a few minutes, looking over the wall and then, with a quick glance at the other guests who were busy talking, he slid out through an opening between two bushes and was immediately lost from my sight.

Good riddance, I said to myself, good riddance even at the cost of a bottle of wine. I was glad that neither child had noticed the man going as they were too busy peering at the French ship and practising trying to say, '*Bonjour, Monsieur*' or '*Voulez-vous du gateau?*' without dissolving into giggles. The man to whom Uncle Timmy had been talking, Simon Ainsworth, came across to join our little group. I looked at him curiously. He was a nice fellow, usually rather an easy-going man but now after he had greeted me and said a few words to the children, I noticed that his eyes, which had followed the direction where Uncle Timmy had gone, before turning back to me, were full of anger and his lips were compressed. He wore, I thought, the expression of a man who was, with difficulty, mastering a feeling of intense anger, and after he had found a few sweets in his pocket for the children who had gone back to speculating about the French ship, I could not resist trying to find out a little more about the man to whom he had been talking.

'Comes from Ireland, that fellow, doesn't he?' I said, jerking a thumb in the direction of the cliff. There was now no sign of Uncle Timmy, but that was not surprising as the cliff was closely covered with clumps of brambles and numerous bushy clusters of blackthorn, interspersed with the mounds of yellow sandy soil deposited by the convicts' buckets. It was a place where a man could be lost from sight quite quickly. He would be no loss to our company, but I saw the faces of his three nephews turned in the direction from where he had vanished from sight. And Georgina, also, had stopped eating and sat with a piece of cake in one hand and the other shielding her eyes as she, also, stared across the marsh. This man created an atmosphere of unease even during those hugely animated conversations which normally characterized Dickens' outdoor meals.

'I wouldn't know,' said Simon, abruptly, replying to my question after a few moments of silence and then with a sidelong glance at me, he continued, 'Never saw the man before, though now that you mention it, he does have an Irish accent. First time in my life seeing him,' he added, as though to strengthen his statement. Not an accomplished liar, I thought. Even a ten-year-old would have noticed the note of embarrassment in his voice. And the men knew each other – had had previous dealings. I was sure of that. And I was equally sure that Simon, who was a friend to everyone, did not like the man. I didn't question him, though. If Uncle Timmy was really a moneylender, then not many people would want to acknowledge a friendship with him. Simon was an actor, quite a good actor, he got many parts as the 'handsome-young-man-around-town' but unfortunately these parts were usually minor ones and not very well paid. It was, I had heard, hard to make a living wage as an actor unless you were a star and, even then, there were often lean months. And for an actor, no matter how well you were paid, the wage was always unsure and liable to come at widely spaced intervals during the year. The chance of young Simon needing the services of a moneylender like our fellow guest, from time to time, were, I guessed, quite strong. And from what I had heard of this unpleasant man he did not hesitate to use his power over his victims, forcing the surrender of valuable possessions to avoid persecution.

'I heard that you were great as Barnardo in that dress-rehearsal of *Hamlet* – Macready, himself, told me that.' I said to Simon, encouragingly. And added, 'I bet you will be chosen for the part and will get some good notices in the papers once it opens to the public.'

He sighed. I noticed that. 'If only I could get paid for dress rehearsals,' he said. 'Or else stop eating,' he added as, with a wave of his hand, he turned and went away. I noticed that his shoulders were bent and that his head was hanging down and I felt very sorry for him. A nice fellow, very easy-going, but one who would allow matters to build up to an intolerable degree before he could rouse himself to take decisive action.

By now, everyone had eaten and drunk their fill, and the baskets were being loaded with dishes and with untouched food, while the leftovers were sprinkled upon the rocks for the seabirds to feed upon. Carrie took a fancy to this unusual way of clearing up after a meal. Grabbing Plorn by the hand, she flew off to lend her services and I made my way towards where Dickens stood. Unusually for him, he was not organizing the clearing away of the meal, but was standing, cigar in hand and looking pensively at the buckets filled with heavy yellow clay travelling up and down the pulley.

'Amazing what man's ingenuity can invent, Collins, is it not?' he said, once he realized that I was standing beside him. 'Think of the terrible effort it would be for these poor fellows, these convicts, to carry those terribly heavy buckets to the top of the hill, but the great Plutarch put his mind to work and invented the pulley. Now all they need are the rope and the metal grooves and hey presto, the weight of one bucket going down, pulls the other bucket up! The only effort that mankind needs is to tug a few feet of rope just to start the process and then up and down they go like clockwork. Now why can't they arrange that the digging of the floor of the seashore can be done by mechanical means? Unquestionably, that's not beyond the scope of man's brain, don't you agree?' he added, appealing to his audience with the customary Dickensian air of sure and certain knowledge that all would agree with him. I noted with amusement that the guests were nodding vigorously while someone even ventured upon a 'Hear, hear!'

'Rubbish,' said Henry Burnett. As usual, he never hesitated to disagree with his famous brother-in-law, even if he were the only one to do so. 'Rubbish,' he repeated. 'I suppose that you would have convicts sitting before a fire and smoking a cigar, serving their sentence, while the machines did all the work, wouldn't you? And then when they finished their sentence they would go off and break into another unfortunate poor man's house and steal all his goods. Or else meet a man on a dark night and rob him of all that he possesses. You need to give these scoundrels a sentence that will make them vow never to do wrong again because they fear the consequences of what will happen if they do so. Don't you agree, Collins?' he said, appealing to me as I had a reputation of arguing with Dickens.

I was spared the necessity of replying as Dickens himself was well-briefed with facts and figures and regaled us all with the number who do re-offend, no matter how harsh the conditions like these unfortunates working in the freezing cold, up to their knees in seawater, from morning to night and then living in the cold and damp of those old hulks. 'I'd have them work – work is good for all of us; I despise lazy, idle people who try to live off others,' he said emphatically, with a glance at his brother-in-law who, I remembered hearing, was somewhat inclined to borrow money from his famous brother-in-law. Dickens gave his words time to sink in before continuing, 'But I would have them taught a trade so that when they are released from prison, they will be able to get a job with a good wage and not be tempted to go back into a life of crime. Hard work is good for us all so long as it leads to a satisfactory result.'

There was, I felt, an uneasy atmosphere among the guests. Most were highly conventional, law-abiding citizens who would not dream of upsetting the present laws and customs for dealing with those who broke the law. Dickens, when the humour seized him, could be very radical about changing the status quo and I rather thought that this was not the time nor place for a political argument. I decided to change the subject and remove Dickens from his brother-in-law. I touched him on the shoulder.

'Come on, Dick, let's walk over to the village,' I said impulsively.

I could just see the village in the distance across the marshes. Not too far, but just far enough to make a walk that would pleasantly fill the rest of the after-lunch period and would be another experience before we went home to Dickens' hospitable house. Moreover, the air was getting colder, and a brisk walk would do everyone good and allow small groups of like-minded persons to chat to each other. I reminded myself that it was still midwinter although days were now beginning to lengthen. The light was beginning to fade, and the marshes were just a long black horizontal line, fenced in by the gleaming line of the river and above it all, the pale blue sky had begun to turn to an ominous purple shade.

'Let's go,' I said decisively, seizing Carrie's hand. She was a good little walker for her age, and I planned to keep her occupied looking out for the gleaming silver-white of the sea stones which were placed over the most soggy parts of the original marsh. There was a well-marked path where the villagers came, to and fro, to their church every Sunday and saints days of their lives, a path which twisted in and out, avoiding the clumps of bulrushes and small ponds and thereby making for a more interesting walk than a dull, straight, concrete road.

Carrie, at any rate was intrigued by this wandering path and we set off walking it merrily, glad to have a very visible target like the tree-lined village to direct our footsteps. It had a certain novelty this walk, not like a normal track through the countryside, but more of a twisty irregular passage through that dark, flat wilderness, intersected with dikes and mounds and gates and with scattered cattle feeding upon juicy clumps of grass and clambering over the rough knolls to reach the most desirable of the tufts.

'Let's see how quickly we can get to the beacon,' I said to

Carrie. It made a good landmark, that beacon, standing like
an unhooped cask upon a pole, not too far away from where
we were and to pass the time, I told Carrie the sailors would
look out for that beacon when they had crossed the sea and
were bringing exciting boxes full of treasure back to London
from places like India.

'When they see the beacon, they know they are going the
right way towards London, a city full of shops and shopkeepers
who want to buy their goods,' I finished and waited for her
questions.

'What's that other thing, the thing with the chains hanging
down, is that a beacon, too?' she wanted to know, and I
pondered over what explanation I could give for a pirate's
gibbet and how I could shield her from the knowledge of that
agonizing fate of a human being, chained there until he died
from exposure and from starvation.

'If someone is very bad, and they steal from ships, they
have to stand there until they are good again,' I said after a
few minutes' thought, and hoped that she would believe me.

'We have a special chair like that in school,' she told me
in a satisfied fashion. 'If you are naughty you have to sit on
that until you say sorry.'

'Yes, a bit like that,' I said with relief and looked up at the
sea. Soon the evening star would appear, I told her and added
that the first person to see it might have a sweet from my
pocket. And so, she fixed her attention on the sky, holding
my hand so that she did not trip over a stone while she was
looking upwards. I saw that the cattle were lifting their heads
and wondered how they spent their nights in this lonely and
desolate spot.

'Look, Carrie,' I said. 'We're walking so fast that we are
coming nearer and nearer to the village.' I hoped that it would
not take too much longer. The sky seemed to be getting dark
more quickly than I had expected, and we might, I feared, be
forced to turn back before reaching our goal.

As the first houses set amongst the alder trees appeared in
the distance I called out to Dickens. 'Who is going to see the
village first! Will it be Plorn or Carrie?'

And, of course, as I had expected, when the village came

within sight, both children called out instantly and so both
were the winners.

'Let's go back and find the others and tell them that we
saw the village,' I said.

'Frank and Walter will be so cross,' said Plorn happily and
so Carrie declared that all the grown-ups would be so cross,
also. Cheerfully competing with memories of names, both
children turned around without argument and passed the time
guessing what everyone would say as Dickens and I cast
anxious glances into the sky until we came within seeing
distance of the door of the small church. We were at the gate
into the churchyard when suddenly the heavens opened, and
thick snow began to fall. Without hesitation I snatched up
Carrie and began to run for the church door. Dickens and
Plorn, hand in hand, overtook us and I was conscious of a
feeling of relief when I pushed open the door and saw that
the little church was full of people.

There looked to be quite a dense crowd there, but when we
came near Walter called out to his father, 'Your visitor from
Cork isn't here. None of his nephews know where he is.
Everyone else is here, I think. I counted heads a while ago.'

They were all there, the nephews, all clustered together,
almost defensively, I thought, and I wondered at their worried
expressions and at the way they exchanged covert glances with
each other.

'He's dead,' said Carrie solemnly. 'I see'd him. I see'd him
when we were running into the church. He's dead and he's
lying on the grave.'

I hushed her quickly by the infallible method of popping a
sweet into her mouth. I was annoyed to see that there was
a frightened expression on the faces of the nephews of the
missing man. Surely they realized that Carrie was a small
child who liked to attract attention by saying outrageous
things.

'He's probably found shelter somewhere,' I said, but even
as I uttered the words, they sounded improbable to my own
ears. Apart from the church, there was no shelter on this bleak
marsh, unless the man had gone to the village. And if he had,
surely we would have seen him. None of his nephews, I noticed,

made any move towards the door, though that would have been the expected action if they really were worried about him.

'Anyway,' I said in a light-hearted way, 'he is a grown man. He can look after himself.'

I addressed my cheerful words to the cluster of nephews, but they didn't have the expected reaction of relief and slight embarrassment. Swayne looked at Caleb; Bypers looked at them both. Long looks and then all of the young men looked down at their hands, each appearing to copy the other's gesture. They were, I reckoned, so browbeaten by their uncle that they found it difficult to have a normal reaction to any unexpected happening. If little Carrie or Plorn were missing from the crowd within the church, why then it would have been natural for everyone to be concerned, but surely such a reaction was ridiculous when it came to the absence of a grown man in a snow shower. Their unease, though, seemed to infect the other guests and the jolly atmosphere had begun to melt rapidly away and to be replaced by an odd feeling of puzzled apprehension as though Dickens' guests felt that something threatening had taken over the Christmas atmosphere that had previously prevailed.

After about twenty minutes had elapsed, minutes which everyone passed by wandering around the church and reading out the inscriptions penned for the dead clergy of the parish, we were disturbed by the sound of a foghorn.

'The French ship must be moving,' I said to Carrie who was getting bored and restive. 'Let's go and have a look. Perhaps the snow is stopping.'

'Good idea!' Dickens, in his own way, was as restless as any child. The little church was well known to him as he had probably walked there on many occasions and doubtless had escorted numerous house parties to see the strange grave with its effigies of the dead children. Now he wanted a change. And, of course, where Dickens led, all followed. So, a few moments later we were all outside the church admiring the sprinkling of snow that turned the marshland into a gleaming white landscape. The crowd of men and the few women exclaimed with excitement and admiration as they gazed around, using a hand to shield eyes against the dazzling snow.

It was exciting and Christmas-like and I could feel that spirits rose rapidly.

But it was Dickens who saw the body. My eyes were fixed upon the unfortunate convicts who still, despite the snow, were drearily filling buckets with the yellow sandy soil from beneath the sea. One man, I noticed, received a cut of the overseer's whip when attracted by Dickens' shout he put down his spade and turned to look in our direction. Another was hastily reeling one of the buckets back to its correct place while looking anxiously over his shoulder at the man with the whip.

And then I forgot about the convicts. Dickens' voice, calling to his son, was clear as a bell. 'Quick, Frank,' he shouted. 'Get Pat. There's a man lying on the cliff edge over there.'

I could see what he was pointing at now. No convict. This man, lying on the cliff slope, wearing that distinctive jacket in a lurid shade of yellow, was unmistakable. By now we had been joined by the others from the little church and his three nephews must have instantly recognized the distinctive figure. Even from that distance I think that everyone recognized from the immobility of the figure that we were looking not at a living body, but at a dead man.

What was immensely strange was that not one of the three nephews made a move to go to examine the corpse of their uncle. Nor did they exchange glances. In fact, they appeared to avoid each other's gaze. The brothers stood very straight, each peering into the distance, each looking in the direction where the man lay on the cliffside.

As usual, Dickens took control. A quick glance over the assembled crowd, an immediate rejection of the females and the overweight, rotund figure of Simon Ainsworth and fastened upon me.

'Come on, Collins,' he said.

I quickly placed Carrie within the arms of Georgina, who was standing near to me. Georgina was white-faced and trembling and it would distract her to have Carrie to care for. I saw how Carrie immediately took an interest in Georgina's diamond necklace, so I left her quite happily and went as quickly as possible to where Dickens and his two sons were standing. Even when I arrived within touching distance of them, I still spoke in hushed tones.

'Is he dead?' I asked.

A stupid question, I told myself as soon as the words had passed my lips. Of course, the man must be dead. Even from a distance we had seen the terrible wound to the skull and when we approached the corpse, the mixture of blood and oozing brains made me turn my head away and hope that I would not vomit. I clenched my hands, concentrating on digging my fingernails into the palms of my hands, trying desperately to distract myself from the terrible sight. Of course, the man was dead, and no one bothered to reply to my question. I stood passively and waited for Dickens to deal with the situation.

# SEVEN

D ickens, as usual, had the matter well in hand and his quick brain produced a task for each of us. Frank was to take the horse from the cart and go as quickly and safely as he could to summon the police and report the tragic death – 'death' said Dickens with a stern eye upon his son who nodded obediently and repeated the two words: 'tragic death'. And then Frank was to go to Gad's Hill and return with another pair of horses and the large carriage so that all could be quickly conveyed home to be looked after by his wife and his sons. Dickens, once all was well with his guests, would return here and meet the police at the scene of the murder.

In the meantime, Walter was to stay at that spot and make sure that no one approached the body until the police arrived. Dickens was going to break the news to the whole party and to propose that they walk to the picnic spot and then when everyone was warm with the exercise, they might, once again, take refuge in the church. I was left with the unpleasant task of confronting the prison guards from the hulks with the distasteful news that a man lay dead and that a convict or more probably several of his convicts were probably guilty of the murder of one of Charles Dickens' Christmas guests. And then, he suggested that I might like to join Walter who was to stand by the dead body and not to move from it until the police arrived. And with that Dickens surveyed his minions, gave a quick nod as he saw Frank ride off at high speed, and went off to his own task, leaving myself, and Walter to follow his instructions.

I wished that he had tackled the prison ship guards himself. I think that he would have managed the matter better. I was clumsy about it and caused offence to the guards, one of whom handed a pair of glasses to me. I was told to survey the convicts and to bear witness to the fact that every single one of them was under the eye of a prison guard and I was asked whether I had any suggestions on how to do the job better.

And so, having listened as politely as I could to the indignation of the prison guard and his assertions that he never took his eye off any of his charges, I went back to keep Walter company. Dreary work and a dreary place. We both, I thought, without saying anything, were envying Frank who was galloping along the road entrusted with two missions which could be easily fulfilled. We would, I knew, soon be cheered by the arrival of Pat's second-in-command driving the carriage to take the ladies back to Gad's Hill and perhaps leading a few horses for those gentlemen who wanted to get back quickly to Dickens' hospitable home. However, we two, I understood from Dickens, were doomed to our awful vigil until the body was surrendered to the possession of the police.

'Can't wait to get away from this place. Never liked it,' said Walter. 'When we were younger, Frank and I used to plan to blow up the church and graveyard so that we could never again have to spoil our Christmas by being dragged over here with his unfortunate guests. What a place for a Christmas expedition! Enough to make anyone commit a murder,' he added flippantly and then threw up his hands apologetically as I frowned upon him.

'How was he killed, do you think?' I asked as we both stared down upon the corpse and at the clotted blood upon the broken head.

Walter, a thoughtful boy who was now looking slightly abashed, took his time over answering and when he did, his reply was slightly off the point. 'My father wanted me to become a doctor at one stage,' he said eventually. 'To be honest, Wilkie, I really didn't think that I had the brains for it, but looking at that mess, I'm glad that he gave up that ambition. Imagine spending your days staring at sights like this and being expected to do something about it.'

I shuddered slightly and averted my eyes. 'To be fair to your father,' I said eventually, 'and I do know what he demands of friends and sons, but I don't think that even he would have expected you to do something about that man's skull. What he needs is a gravedigger, not a doctor.'

Walter grinned at my feeble joke and we both began to feel better. With one accord, we turned our backs upon the corpse and the bloodstained snow, rubbing our frozen hands and executing a sort of Morris dance to warm our feet.

'If Frank were here, he would be forcing me to place a bet upon it. We'd go through all the guests, and he'd persuade me to bet on one and he would bet on the another,' said Walter. 'He's a great fellow for betting – don't tell my father. He would have a fit. Frank would find himself with his allowance cut off. My father was angry enough when he, also, refused to be a doctor – after I escaped by going to sea, my father's ambition turned to Frank. He even offered to tutor him for the entrance examination. And nothing in the world is as nerve-wracking as being tutored by my father – except, perhaps, having to ask him for money.'

I said nothing to that. I wondered whether Walter had been quite honest with me when he said that he never borrowed from a moneylender as, so far, his father had always provided funds when he needed them. It didn't, I thought, sound like Dickens. And Dickens' sons were rather in awe of him and would probably prefer not to have to ask for a loan. Dickens, I knew, was determined that his sons would become self-supporting as soon as possible and was not inclined to indulge them. He continually reminded them that he had been sent out to earn a living when he was a child of barely twelve years old. I did hope that Walter had not dealt with money-lenders, or more importantly, I had to say to myself, with that one moneylender who now lay dead on this bleak marshland.

I found myself shivering violently – from the cold, perhaps, but also from feelings of deep apprehension. This was going to be a most unpleasant business. Unless the police managed to pin the murder upon one of the convicts, poor devils, it had to be one of Dickens' guests, or even perhaps one of his family. Walter and Frank were well-grown boys who exercised violently with balls, bats, tennis rackets and golf clubs as well as walking, running and riding horses. More than any of their father's guests they would be capable of knocking the brains from a sleeping man.

Walter was now silent, most unusually silent for such a garrulous boy, I thought to myself.

'Do you see that track in the grass?' he said eventually. He pointed up to the edge of the graveyard. My eyes followed the direction of his finger and I saw what he meant. The snow from the fall of less than half an hour ago had begun to melt and the cliffside had now reverted to green. There was undoubtedly a flattened track coming down the hill to where we stood and continuing to a thicket of blackthorn at a spot beside the dead body.

'Let's have a search,' he said and with a quick and slightly guilty look at the dead body which he had been told to guard, we both searched around. I wasn't sure what I was looking for – some sort of cudgel, I guessed but Walter seemed to know what he was doing. After a couple of minutes, he leaped over a hillock of wet soil and thrust an arm into the depths of a clump of blackthorn.

'That's it, Wilkie,' he said triumphantly. 'Look at it. There's your murderer!'

I started, but there was a broad grin on his face, so I regained my courage and joined him.

At first, I couldn't quite see anything except a pile of shattered twigs beside a flat rock, but then I realized what had happened. Lodged into the broken bush was a long object, a rounded shape, murky white and though half buried over by the vegetation there was no mistaking it. It was the effigy of a child, one of the pathetic gravestones in the form of a small angel from the sad little grave of those children who had probably died of marsh fever.

'The wound on the head,' I said slowly.

'Hit on the forehead with that weight, he wouldn't have had a chance,' said Walter.

'But . . .' I said stupidly, looking down at the clump of limestone. I reached down and touched it. How had it got from the graveyard down the hill and smashed the man's head? And having done that, how could it have rolled on down the hill until it was stopped by the blackthorn bush?

'Someone was up there, up in the churchyard,' said Walter. 'Saw him sitting down here, at the bottom of the hillside, sheltering from the wind. There's a half-smoked cigar on the ground there, beside the body. He probably bent down to light it again and the person up there, the person watching him, tipped over the statue, sent it rolling down the hill. Or else he was asleep there. That's the most likely. He drank enough at lunch time to knock out any normal man and then he went off with another bottle under his arm. I saw him. He walked back here, then he sat down and finished the bottle. He may have been asleep, or even if he were not, he wouldn't have been in a condition to notice much. It's thick grass there. He would not have heard the stone rolling until it was too late. Hit him on the head and killed him immediately.'

I thought about it. Walter was a practical boy, a sailor who was doing well in the Navy. I was sure that he was right. The man that we had known as 'Uncle Timmy', had met his death from the carved effigy which mourning parents had placed upon the grave of one of the dead children of the marshland.

'But . . . but who?'

My words lingered on the air for a minute before he replied, and I looked nervously around. A man who had killed once would kill again. I was glad that I had the sturdily built Walter with me. There was something eerie about this place.

'It must have been an accident, a terrible accident,' I said, trying to sound as though I believed my own words.

'No accident!' said Walter with a note of scorn in his voice. He pointed towards the top of the hill. 'Look up there,' he said. 'Someone made that hole in the wall. It wasn't there earlier. You can see how he, or even she, stacked the stones of that wall of the churchyard and then tipped the gravestone, the little statue, out of the grave, sending it rolling through the space that he had made and down the hill. Look up there! If the wall stones had been scattered by the lump of stone it might possibly have been an accident, but that would have made a lot of noise and perhaps woken a sleeping man. No, the stones were taken quietly out, one by one, stacked to one side and then the stone statue of the child was rolled off the grave and was sent rolling down the hill to where a man lay sleeping. Yes, he probably was asleep. So, he was a sitting duck. Someone who had a grudge, saw him there and rolled the stone statue down and killed him.'

I thought about it and felt sure that he was right.

'But who killed him if it wasn't an accident?' I said slowly. 'Do you know anything about him, Walter?'

He did not answer. Just looked at me sideways. He had heard something about this man, had picked up a few hints; I was sure of that. I wondered whether he had any idea of who had dealt the fatal blow, but he said no more about the identity of the dead man. He was a boy who kept his own council. Now he returned to an examination of the body.

'Wouldn't have taken too much strength,' he said, and I realized the significance of the words. Man or woman could have done the deed. One push from the grave and onto that steep, smooth surface and the statue would have rolled, gathering momentum as it went down the slope. There was no doubt that the statue would have killed a man. A man lying there sunk into a drunken sleep would not, could not, have heard the stone rolling on the thick grassy surface of that very steep hill, not, at least, before it was too late to escape. I looked away from the broken head and the blood-stained face and fixed my eyes upon the river and the two convict hulks.

'Each one of them holds about five hundred convicts,' said Walter at my shoulder. 'So, I've been told, but I suppose they die off at quite a rate and then they drop the body into the water, so I've heard. But there may have been up to a thousand convicts working here on the side of the river. Be a job to know one from the other, wouldn't it? All of them dressed the same. The police will have quite a job cross-questioning them, won't they?'

'Them?' I queried.

'Well, it's a going to be a convict, isn't it? My father has said so, hasn't he?'

He had a strange expression on his face. A very cynical look. Not much more than the age of twenty, I would have thought, but already that cynical look. Dickens' sons, once past their idyllic early childhood, were brought up to be tough.

'Funny business, last night, that game, wasn't it?' he said and then with a nod of his head towards the body on the ground, he said, 'Asked some funny questions, that fellow, didn't he? And those addresses, had them off pat, didn't he?'

'I didn't really notice,' I said evasively. He was right, of course. There was something odd and threatening about the way in which the dead man had produced addresses. Walter's own father, Charles Dickens, usually so relaxed and amused, had shown quite a strange reaction when he had heard O'Connor mention forty-five Grafton Street, but I wasn't going to discuss that with Walter. Dickens was supersensitive about certain matters and Walter was by no means his favourite son. 'No,' I said in the tone of one who wanted to change the conversation, 'no, I really didn't notice anything strange about the addresses.'

'Ah, but you are squeaky clean, Wilkie, aren't you,' said the bumptious young man. 'He was a moneylender, wasn't he? Had information about a lot of people there last night, don't you think? But not you, of course. Nothing to do with you, was he? Never borrowed a penny in your life, did you, Wilkie? Came into the world with a silver spoon in your mouth, just two of you, yourself and your brother for your father to finance – not like my father with ten of us – and now, even after your father has died, you have no troubles, do you? After all, he left plenty of money in the bank, didn't he? And now, even if your own money is running short, you have a mother to provide anything you need, don't you? It has been a different matter with a lot of the guests last night; I can tell you that, Wilkie. You must have noticed the atmosphere when that fellow, now lying dead at our feet, the way he was taking down the details about my father's guests. Those questions, those addresses, the information about them that he seemed to want to know. You must have noticed the reaction. Tense as anything, the atmosphere, wasn't it, Wilkie? Quite surprised me, he did. Wonder what the significance of that mention of a blacking factory was that he mentioned to my father? What do you think, Wilkie? Didn't you notice the great man's reaction?'

I wasn't going to discuss my friend Dickens with his son

and so I pursed my mouth into an expression of disbelief and
then smiled patronizingly upon him.

'You make me feel old,' I said disagreeably. 'I just about
remember being your age and loving to make a mystery out
of everything.'

He laughed cheerfully with the air of one who was not to
be diverted from his conclusions. 'Well, you can't say that
everything is my imagination. After all, we have a mystery
lying at our feet, don't we, Wilkie?' he said. 'The last time that
we saw that statue, it was up there on top of a grave and the
graveyard was surrounded by stones. The statue itself, even to
someone with my father's imagination, could not have come
to life; could not have made that large hole in the wall and
could not have piled the stones beside it. The statue, by
itself, could not have moved itself off the soil of the grave
and gone hurtling down the hill to smash the brains out of a
man's head, now could it, Wilkie? Someone did it, Wilkie.
Someone, man or woman, someone opened a gap in that wall;
someone rolled that statue; someone killed that man, and I
think that they did it to shut his mouth. Someone did not like
the hints that he was dropping last night while pretending to
play a game. Someone felt threatened by him and when they
saw him lying there, snoring, probably after all that wine he
had consumed, then they were tempted to get rid of him
with no risk to themselves. Quickly and neatly done, I'd say.
And it might be hard, very hard indeed, to discover who did it.
Difficult to see where people were on this hillside, wasn't
it, Wilkie? I'm sure that you noticed that, didn't you? All these
bushes and all these humps and hollows would make it almost
impossible to tell where everyone was, man . . . or woman,'
he added with his eyes fixed upon me.

I wished that he had not said that last word. Georgina had
come to my mind. Her passionate hatred for the man and her
terror that he would betray her, or worse, make her a pauper.
Due to her reckless borrowing, she was at his mercy, and she
appeared to have no way of escaping him. Could a woman
commit a violent crime like that? Physically, yes. Walter was
right about that. The stones in the wall were not impossible
to lift. The hole could have been made by a woman, even by

a child. And after the hole was made, everything was easily done. One push and the stone statue would progress under its own momentum. Georgina could have done that deed, could have given the initial push, and then stood back. Had Walter noticed her tears during her conversation with me on the previous evening? Had he observed her abhorrence when the moneylender tried to sit beside her at dinnertime? He may not have been academic, but Walter had all his father's sharpness and interest in people.

'Or it could have been one of the convicts, of course,' I said, but my voice lacked conviction. It was all very well for Dickens to mention the convicts, but why on earth should any of them want to kill a man that they had probably never seen before in their lives. And every move that the convicts made was watched by their guards. Somehow, I doubted whether a convict would have been able leave his work and go into the church graveyard for long enough to send that stone rolling down the hill. Even a momentary deviation from the dreary routine of digging out the sandy earth from under the river, filling the buckets and depositing them upon the marsh, was followed mercilessly by harsh shouts and the cracking of the whips. And the convicts were shackled and chained. Not easy for them to slip out of sight.

And, even if they had slipped away unnoticed, what could have been the motive?

No gain was possible, not while they were convicts.

But could it have been revenge?

Yet, what relationship could exist between a convict and a businessman?

Unless, of course, the dead man had perhaps, sometime in the past, employed one of those convicts, cheated him or, worse still, was responsible for his imprisonment and for the dreary life that he now led as a convict who was treated worse than any slave. My mind began to concoct a story where a gang of thieves and murderers had been under the control of the unsavoury Irishman. It was an interesting thought. A very possible way of accumulating a lot of money. After all, after a burglary, the police usually concentrated on those who lived near to the property or on thieves well-known to them. Uncle

Timmy, as I still called him in my mind, because of his business premises in London and his dwelling place in Cork, could rapidly leave the place of the crime and slip between England and Ireland without causing any curiosity.

It would, I felt, be a huge weight off my mind if I could deflect the attention of the police from Dickens' Christmas guests and encourage them to concentrate on the history of the convicts who were present in the place of the murder. The tearstained face of poor Georgina came to me, and I resolved to do my best for her.

Aloud, I said, 'Did you know him, Walter? He was a money-lender, wasn't he? Did you, did you . . .' I hesitated to finish but it was in my mind that young men, especially sociable young men like Walter, often did overspend and then needed the service of a moneylender.

He shook his head vigorously. 'Not me, Wilkie. So far, I've steered clear of moneylenders, and up to now I've managed to tap into the paternal bank – a humble begging letter to my dear father, filled with promises of reform, of course, has so far not gone unanswered, though he had warned me that his patience is running low. But he even financed me coming home for Christmas. Likes his Christmas celebrations, does my dearly beloved father and Charley has let him down this year. Leaving here as soon as he can and spending Christmas Day with the family of his young lady. My father is not pleased. Doesn't like the family of Charley's young lady – Charley's future father-in-law used to be my father's publisher and, as you know, Wilkie, they quarrelled. And now the famous author's son wants to marry the publisher's daughter. You can imagine, Wilkie, how that went down with my father,' said Walter. 'And so, he fell back on me, your humble servant, son number two.' Walter gave a cynical grin and turned back to look down upon the dead man, while I mused upon the people whom the dead man had appeared to target.

'I don't see your father murdering a guest,' I said aloud, and Walter laughed.

'Ah, but you are under the spell, Wilkie. I don't believe that you would hear a word said against him.'

'Nor would you,' I said and watched
across his face.

'No, I don't suppose that I would, the
said cheerfully, and continued, 'In fact, I wo
a murder for him if I felt that it would be in
After all, you know, Wilkie, the whole famil\
upon him. Even out in India or Australia, my you.
will get positions just because they are sons of
author, Charles Dickens, who is already planning po.
the poor little buggers. I don't suppose that I would ha
made a lieutenant at my age and with my lack of tale
had not been the son of that same famous novelist wh
give him his due, wrote lots of very well-expressed letters
my behalf.'

There was an odd cynical note in his voice which discon-
certed me, and I was pleased to hear the clip-clop sound of
horses' hoofs, accompanied by men's voices.

'Here they come,' I said relieved to be terminating our
previous conversation. 'It's your father with the police. And
Frank. Your brother has made good time – he was a good
choice to send for the police.'

'Frank is the best rider of us all. My father,' said Walter,
still with that odd and cynical note in his voice, 'does everything very well and very efficiently. Yes, of course, he would
make a good choice and yes, of course, Frank would not
disappoint him but would make very good time.'

I ignored this and raised an arm to direct Dickens to the
spot where we stood in guard over the dead body.

# EIGHT

Dickens, as usual, had the air of conferring a great pleasure on both parties as he made the introductions.

'Sergeant Jones. And, Sergeant, this is Mr Wilkie Collins, the novelist.'

As we shook hands with an assumed air of mutual pleasure, Dickens waved a hand towards Walter.

'And this,' he said in an offhand fashion, 'is one of my many boys. Can't remember his name at the moment – there are too many of them to find room in my poor brain.'

The sergeant gave a slightly embarrassed nod in our direction and Walter grinned. Dickens' sons got used to their father's many jokes about his large family and rarely showed signs of resenting his jokes.

'I'm son number two, Father,' he said smartly. 'Name of Walter. At your service, Sergeant.' He held out a hand and grinned happily at the rather uncomfortable man.

'Well, it was Walter who found what killed the dead man,' I said to cover my own slight embarrassment. 'Show them, Walter.'

The sergeant bent over the dead body, lifted an eyelid while feeling the pulse and then made a quick note before turning back to Walter.

'At your service, now, sir,' he repeated Walter's words smartly, and Walter led the way up towards the wall around the little churchyard, followed by the two men. I stayed where I was and looked across the marshes. A faint mist was rising from the damp clumps of vegetation. The air had become warmer, and I hoped that it was not a sign of snow. I wanted to get away from this dreary spot and to get back to the warmth and cheer of Gad's Hill. There would be, of course, no going back to the happy, cheerful atmosphere of the preceding day. Unless, of course, the sharp-eyed inspector would be content to take the easy way out and immediately assign blame to the convicts. That, I felt, might be the easiest solution for us and for a few minutes I consoled myself with the thought, but then came back to a realization that the convicts, just like Dickens' guests, were human beings. It might be initially convenient if the police turned their suspicions to them, but it probably meant a lot of savage whippings of these unfortunate fellows to get information out of them, whereas Dickens' guests would be carefully and politely questioned until suspicions grew to near certainty. And, in addition the burden of proof, in the case of the convicts, might be taken lightly so, quite possibly, an innocent man might be hanged for the murder of a person whom he had never met.

No, I thought. I should not take the easy way out but would put my energies to unravelling this problem. *The Times* had praised my new book, *The Moonstone*; had admired the mystery at its core and had suggested, to my slight embarrassment, that it should be mandatory reading for any policeman who had the crime of murder to solve.

So, I, Wilkie Collins, the author of *The Moonstone* who, while writing books had mentally explored the mind of a criminal, had acquired, perhaps, a knowledge of how to weigh suspicions, probe motives and assess probabilities. I would put my brain to work, would use my inside knowledge of Dickens' guests, and come to an accurate decision about who was the murderer. I could not bear that thought of some poor convict who might even be innocent of his original crime, being forced into a false confession by the torture of the whip. It was, I thought, far more likely that one of the guests had devised this clever way of murdering a man who might pose a threat to them. It would have been a very clever murder and it would be hard to convict anyone of setting the stone statue rolling. The perfect murder, perhaps. It could be blamed upon the hand of God.

The atmosphere in Dickens' hospitable house on this Christmas holiday had been marred from the very beginning, marred by the presence of this Timmy O'Connor, the man who had whispered in ears and who was now dead. Many of Dickens' guests had appeared to have known this man, this lender of money who tormented his victims and divested them of large portions of their inherited money. I would, I thought, be able to find half a dozen with possible motives – enough to confuse the police, to distract them from the unfortunate convicts and to keep them focused on an almost impossible task of sifting through the background of all of Dickens' guests on that Christmas morning.

I could, also, in addition, I thought, point out that we had made a lot of noise on our arrival and that it was eminently possible for a thief and murderer to be lurking in the background and to seize upon the one man in the jolly crowd who appeared to have no friends and who went off to roam the marshes by himself.

Yes, I thought, with a compassionate memory of my dear friend Georgina, who was being blackmailed and harassed by the scoundrel, there were doubtless, many people present who roamed these marshes on this festive day who would be glad to see the end of the moneylender and tormentor. And if I could supply the police with a large group of suspects, why then I would muddy the waters for them and hopefully no one would suffer for that impulse to rid themselves of the man who was torturing them. It could be man or woman, young or old. After all, it probably just took twenty seconds of desperation to set off that fatal rolling of the statue which was to crush the life out of a scoundrel and a blackmailer.

I got to my feet and awaited the return of the sergeant who had now been joined by his inspector, and mentally practised my approach to them.

'You are quite a good actor, Wilkie,' my friend, Charles Dickens, had said to me recently. And the fact that he said the words with a note of grudging reluctance in his voice had made the praise all the more precious to me. Dickens, I knew, despite his wonderful success as a writer, did still, deep down, hanker to be an actor and regarded himself as an expert in that field. If Dickens thought my acting performances were worthy of his jealousy, then it would not take me much effort to deceive a crowd of policemen. I examined them closely as they came back down the hill. The inspector was a redhead

– well that was a good beginning. Most redheads, in my experience, had been so teased and tormented during their school days that they lost all confidence in themselves. I would, I decided, make him my best friend, and bolster his belief in himself while quietly encouraging him along a line of enquiry which would lead him away from any, like poor Georgina, who might be in genuine danger.

So, I brushed the twigs and pieces of dead leaves from my trousers, wiped the traces of damp snow from my hand and advanced to meet the inspector, the events of the last few hours revolving around my mind.

And, of course, I could see instantly that Dickens was the man in charge and that all looked to him for instructions.

Once my friend had fallen in love with the idea of himself as a country squire, he set himself up in that role to become an important person in the neighbourhood, organizing cricket matches and even a sports day that I had witnessed where the local police force competed successfully against their rivals from the town of Chatham. The police inspector, supposedly in charge was, I could see immediately, like putty in the hands of my friend. I waited for them to come near to me and concentrated on removing any trace of a smile from my face and making sure that I looked appropriately solemn.

'My dear Collins,' said Dickens cheerfully, 'I've been lucky enough to find Inspector Gill on duty today – I have spoken to you about Inspector Gill, have I not? – and so, as you can imagine, I feel deeply relieved to know that this unfortunate affair is in such very good hands. Inspector Gill, this is my very good friend, Mr Wilkie Collins. He and I were together throughout the morning, walked over to the village of Cooling, came back together and then, as I was telling you, once the snow began to fall, we took refuge in the church, together, for the whole morning.'

Dickens finished with a slight flourish, and I realized that as well as paying compliments to the policeman he had subtly and judiciously established an alibi for us both and from now on two gentlemen, Mr Dickens and Mr Collins, would be set apart from any suspicion of being involved in the murder of the man whose body lay, sprinkled with snow, not far from where we stood. From now on we were on the side of the police. Tactfully and very carefully, Dickens would guide this Inspector Gill along a predetermined path. I could tell from the slight frown upon my friend's brow and the reflective expression of his eyes, that he was pondering over who might be responsible and who might be the sacrificial goat who would be offered up for the initial police investigation.

Inspector Gill, of course, had immediately jumped to the obvious conclusion. His eyes went to the line of convicts who were digging industriously and ladling the soft sand into their buckets. There was a robotic look to them all. It had been trained into them to work as a team and any attempt to slow down or to move away from the partner assigned to him meant a merciless cut of the whip across the shoulders of an unfortunate man.

Inspector Gill jerked a thumb in their direction.

'These fellows were working nearby at the time, is that right, Mr Dickens?' he asked in a voice which he had successfully made to sound indifferent and unconcerned.

'The convicts? Oh, they've been here for months,' said Dickens. 'I come here quite often, Inspector, and I must say that they are always very carefully supervised, and I would certainly not have brought women and children to this place if I had dreamt that there would have been the slightest danger from their presence. No, the idea that they might be involved did cross my mind, but I think it might be a hard matter to prove, given the measure of supervision which is maintained during the whole time that the prisoners are working on the shoreline. And, of course, Inspector, it would be an enormous coincidence if one of my guests had had anything to do with a convict.'

The inspector grunted an acknowledgement of Dickens' words, but he made no verbal answer, just scribbled a note into his jotter.

'And your own guests, Mr Dickens?'

'Most of my guests, Inspector, are, like Mr Collins here, people of the highest integrity and well known to me over the years. The exceptions, of course, are the dead man and his three nephews. I met up with them in London, after the uncle got in touch with me to say he was visiting. I had enjoyed his hospitality in Cork, so I felt it was only polite to agree to meet them. But then I heard the news about one of the nephews, the twin Tiffen, breaking his leg and being unable to go back home for the Christmas festivities. He is stuck in hospital, poor boy, so, what could I do? I had received such royal hospitality from their native country when I was in Ireland! I could not allow these poor fellows to be stranded in London during the festive season and so, Inspector, and I'm sure that you would have done the same, well, I invited them to spend Christmas in my own house and share in all the merriment that my family devise to entertain their guests.'

'So, you know nothing whatsoever about them,' said Inspector Gill, as he made a few quick notes on his jotter. 'For all you know, they may well have had some sort of connection with one of the convicts working here on the river. Would that be right, sir?'

Dickens hesitated. 'Well, I suppose you could say that.' His tone was reluctant and his words few, but there was little doubt in my mind that he was more than satisfied with the conclusion that the inspector had voiced. The fact of the matter was that Dickens, with his well-known impetuosity, had invited a crowd of men, a man and his three nephews, of whom he knew nothing, to spend Christmas among his family and his friends. And now that man had been murdered here on the marsh and it was quite possible that there had been some long-term enmity between the dead man and one of the convicts. That, to Dickens, would be a much more satisfying conclusion than if the inspector had jumped to the conclusion that there had been an enmity between the dead man and one of the other guests. I did wonder, though, whether that was a possibility, whether, in fact, the presence of the convicts might have been falsely reckoned to provide a convenient screen to obscure the reason for the crime. An opportunist might have seized upon the opportunity to get rid of a man who was harassing him or her for the repayment of a money loan. I waited with a trace of amusement to watch the man of the law jump through the hoops that the famous novelist had set for him.

# NINE

The inspector, however, was quite a shrewd man, or so it appeared to me. I could see how his eyes, filled with speculation, looked out into the turbulent waters of the River Medway. He was turning the facts over in his mind. The dead man, it appeared, was a stranger in the location, a stranger in the county of Kent, a man from across the sea, from that turbulent Irish city of Cork, the second largest city in a country that was continuously at war with its fellow inhabitants. The police inspector compressed his lips, rubbed the chill from his fingers, and then said casually, 'Did they get on well? The uncle and nephews? Did they get on well with each other?'

Dickens allowed a pause of a few minutes to elapse and then, with a shrug of his shoulders, he answered, 'You'll have to talk to them about that, Inspector. I must say that I have no solid evidence, not evidence which would stand up in a court of law – well, you know what it is like . . . you know what families are like! It would,' he said slowly, 'be useful for a man of your experience to speak to these young men, one by one . . .' He left a silence for the inspector to fill mentally before saying lightly, 'I shall be happy to offer you the facilities to conduct your investigations in private and comfortable surroundings back at Gad's Hill.'

I had little doubt that the inspector had previously sampled the comfort of Dickens' house at Gad's Hill and the extent of his hospitality. I could see a spark of anticipation strike a light in the man's eyes and a slight relaxation of the lips.

'That's indeed very kind of you, Mr Dickens,' he said. 'I shall be very pleased to avail myself of your offer and now I think that you should all return to Gad's Hill as quickly as possible. That sky, I must say, looks quite threatening. My sergeant and I will check on the convicts, but I'm sure we will find that the guards here are very careful and conscientious. I've often had occasion to visit the moors and never saw any laxness. We'll follow you and will be back to your house as soon we have done that. Your guests may wish to change and to have some refreshments, a short rest, perhaps, before we arrive, and I have no objection to that.'

My friend gave a satisfied nod of his head and turned his mind to the practicalities.

'You will, of course, want to interview my guests, one by one once you have finished with the convicts and their keepers,' he said to the police officer. 'And, of course, I shall be very pleased to offer you the hospitality of my home to keep you warm and comfortable on this very cold day. I will engage to have a room at your disposal and everyone ready to be interviewed. Let me write you a list of names of those of my family and friends present here with me on the marshes this morning.'

Efficient as always, Dickens tore a sheet of paper from the notebook which he always carried in his breast pocket in case an idea suddenly came to him during one of his long walks. Swiftly and efficiently, he printed out the names.

'Here is a list of the guests not including the children,' he addressed the sergeant who nodded his agreement. I wondered whether Dickens' older sons, such as Walter and Frank, well-grown and strong-looking young men, should be excluded, but it was none of my business, so silently I enumerated the guests upon my fingers and Dickens and I came to an agreement on the ten names, excluding Dickens' sons and my little Carrie. I read them through while Frank was despatched to line up the guests for the homeward journey and to fit the young children and as many visitors as he could manage into Pat's cart while Dickens himself, under the cover of a confidential chat, found a comfortable seat for Jas in the front of the cart next to Pat. The other guests began to walk, assured that the cart would return for them.

Carrie, to my disappointment, made no effort to demand my presence, but was content to be lifted on to Georgina's knee by Frank. A nice boy, Frank. Being one of the eldest of such a large family had given him a caring nature and he, like I, had noticed the pallor on the face of poor Georgina and had quickly found her a place and justified it by plumping Carrie onto her lap.

Dickens looked after the cart with an air of satisfaction. It held some of the ladies, the two young children and a few other guests who were elderly or lacking in vigour. Frank had managed the matter well. And then my friend turned his eyes to me. For a moment I hoped that he might be going to recall his son and tell Frank to find room for me, but he had another matter in his mind.

'I'm sure, Inspector, that you will be interested to hear that my friend here, Mr Collins, the novelist, is planning a new book which will deal with the work of guarding convicts in this interesting part of the world. Would there be any chance that he might stay with you to observe an example of police work at its most accomplished? Would you be able to accommodate him in your vehicle on the way back? And allow him to explain to the great British public how the police work, not only keeping us safe, but also in superintending this wonderful work of extending the river and providing extra room for our ships?'

'Certainly, Mr Dickens, we would be delighted to assist Mr Collins in his literary work!'

'And I would be extremely interested to watch our police and prison warders in action,' I said sedately.

I could see that the inspector was immediately taken by the offer of interviewing the ladies and gentlemen from London in the warmth and privacy of Dickens' house and would, I hoped, spend a minimum of time in interviewing the convicts and the warders. I, eyeing the substantial police conveyance, was equally pleased at the prospect of not just seeing the convicts' ship at close quarters and, of course, of sparing myself a long and dreary walk back. Also, I wondered whether this visit might prove to be the stimulus for a new book. I had read up about the convict ships, but I knew from old that nothing can take the place of that sudden triggering of the imagination brought about by the sight of something that I had never seen before. I would, asserted the policeman, be shown around by the chief warder once on board the ship. He blew a whistle and almost instantly a boat was sent across,

manned by a warder and a couple of sturdy prisoners who
were the oarsmen.

The warder was polite and seemed to be genuinely pleased
to have a visitor. These floating prisons might well prove to
afford a stimulus for my next book, I thought, and so I questioned my escort closely once on board the ship. He proved
to be a mine of information.

'Prison hulks are decommissioned ships,' he told me with
an air of someone who had related these facts so often that
they came readily to his tongue. 'Quite safe in these calm
waters in the harbour,' he assured me, 'but I have to say, sir,
that they would be unfit for going out to sea where they would
be battered by the wind and the waves.'

In the past, I gathered from him, these ships would be broken
up or sold off cheaply, but during the last few decades the
authorities used them as floating prisons. They were mainly
used in calm waters in the English Channel, he told me, and
the term 'prison hulk' was not synonymous with the related
term 'convict ship' as convict ships were the ships used to
take the convicts out to Australia. I knew most of this, of
course, but listened, with feigned interest, as he told me that
a hulk is a ship that is afloat, but incapable of going to sea,
whereas convict ships are seaworthy vessels that transport
convicted felons from their place of conviction to their place
of banishment. Once we were on board, he showed me around
with as much pride as if he had personally built the ship on
purpose to hold convicts.

'A difficult job for you and your men,' I said idly, and added
a compliment about his management skills, saying that the
convicts that I could see were behaving in a very subdued and
orderly fashion.

He appeared pleased with my observation. 'That's thanks
to the Merit Board, sir; they know that my eye is on them,
and they will lose marks if they misbehave. Come and look
at it,' he said with such an air of pride that I was not surprised
when he informed me that this Merit Board was an invention
of his own and when a man accumulated a hundred merit
marks he was brought before the board to be assessed for early
release. No names were written on it – names, on board the

ship, were not encouraged. Each man was distinguished by a letter and a number.

C7, I pointed out to the warder, was doing very well with merit numbers which brought him near to the hundred mark and I wondered facetiously whether his name might be Collins and if so, whether he might be a relative of mine. This mild joke was taken with great exuberance by the warder and number C7 was brought forward to be introduced to me while the warder beamed with pride, like a schoolmaster with a promising pupil.

C7 had a sharp look about him, I thought; the face of a man who would make the best of any situation and I was not surprised that he had worked out the quickest way of getting his sentence shortened. He was full of praise for the inspiration of the warder and described fluently how despairing he had felt when he received his sentence in court.

I was eager to find out about his past life and was turning over in my mind how to make a tactful enquiry, when suddenly his head swivelled around, and his eyes fixed upon a large seagull who had daringly deposited a large and messy dropping on the well-scrubbed deck.

'Excuse me, sir,' said C7 and in a moment he had seized a bucket of water and a scrubbing brush from its position beside the mast and quickly scrubbed the mark away.

'Well done, C7,' said the warder, and then deserting me, he went across to the merit board, used a key from his pocket to open a large wooden box beside it and then dipped a small paint brush into a pot of white paint and added another five marks to the convict's score. Everything was carefully done, I noticed, as the box was relocked, and the key replaced in the warder's pocket after he had checked the lock was firmly in place.

I congratulated C7 and asked him whether he was looking forward to regaining his liberty, wishing him the best of luck.

'Yes, sir, thank you. Not bad places these prison ships, though, gives hope to us prisoners and teaches us to mend our ways,' he said loudly enough to be heard by the warder. Then lowering his voice considerably, he added, 'Not all the worst villains are in prison, sir.'

'I believe you,' I said rapidly. 'The most unlucky, perhaps,' I added to keep the conversation going.

The man did not need my help. He knew what he wanted to say.

'Are you interested in buying a prison ship, yourself, sir?' he asked. Then, without waiting for my answer, he said what was in his mind, 'There was a man here today, speaking to the warder, he was. I've heard that he was the owner of this ship. Bought and sold these prison ships. Moneylender, too. Would lend money to buy a prison ship, so someone told me. Great bargain, these prison ships, so I've heard. Perhaps you know who I am talking about. Saw him here today. Came with your party, today, so he did. That's what gave me the idea that you might be interested in buying a prison ship – a lot of money in it, so they tell me.' He looked at me meaningfully as though awaiting a question.

By now, Dickens had lined up all the guests who were going to walk back with him and had led the way, at a smart pace, out of the precincts of the churchyard. From our position on the ship, we could see the briskly moving line. The convict's eyes followed them.

'Don't see the gentleman there with your party, now, sir,' he said with a note of amusement in his voice. 'Would he have gone home early, do you think? Not from this country, I think. An Irishman by his accent.'

'I know the man of whom you speak, or, at least I knew him when he was alive,' I said slowly and watched the convict's face. There was no trace of puzzlement, nor of genuine surprise upon it.

'Dear, oh dear,' he said with mock astonishment. 'Could it be that the gentleman who was killed was the man who was the owner of this ship?' He gave a hasty look in the direction of the warder and lowered his voice. 'Least said; soonest mended,' he said rapidly and left me abruptly, to chase away another seagull from marring the cleanliness of the deck.

I watched him for a moment, but it didn't seem as though he had anything more to say and so I left him and joined the warder, allowing him to conduct me over the ship, making notes from time to time in my pocketbook, but never ceasing to wonder about that strange man who had met his death here in the desolate churchyard. A moneylender: a man of substance who had sufficient spare money to enable him to buy a prison ship; a man who had cheated his brother's children out of the education and care which their father had hoped to ensure by leaving his money to the brother who was supposed to take the place of a father.

The man was dead now, but who had killed him? He had enemies in plenty. Any one of his three nephews could have avenged himself and his brothers and possibly regained some of the money left for their upbringing; any one of his clients, men or women, to whom he lent money at an outrageous rate, could have decided to get rid of this man who threatened destitution and disgrace to his clients who could not pay back the sums that they had borrowed. And what about those convicts who might have been at his mercy? Could any one of them have been at the end of their tether and fastened upon the owner of the prison ship as being the author of their troubles? A moment's inattention from a warder and one of these convicts could have removed some stones from the drystone wall and sent the heavy statue rolling down the hill towards a sleeping man. It might have worked, and it might not have worked, but in either case it was unlikely that the man who pushed the stone would be observed by the warder. Easy to wait until the man's attention was on something else, the darkening sky, a ship in the distance, one of his fellow warders, trouble with another convict – a moment would be long enough for stones to be removed and the heavy stone to be sent rolling down the steep slope.

'Such a good idea, that merit board of yours,' I said hastily to the warder. 'I wonder whether you could allow me to study it. I don't want to waste your time, so if you would be happy to trust me, I shall just stand here and make some notes as to the progress of the different prisoners.'

I wasn't too sure of what I meant, myself, but the warder beamed at me, and I suspected that I may have been the first outsider to show an interest in this merit board of his.

'Take all the time in the world, sir,' he said earnestly. 'C7, a chair for the gentleman and then take yourself off.' He turned to me. 'I'll make sure that no one disturbs you, sir, but when you have a list of questions for me, then I would be delighted to answer them or to line up some prisoners for you to interrogate – whatever is the most useful for you, sir.'

And so, I was left to myself, sitting on a chair, and examining the merit board while the prison ship rocked gently with the movement of the river.

There would have had to be a very strong reason for any convict to murder the moneylender. It either had to be intense hope – a man whose anticipation of almost imminent release had been threatened, whose release might have been interfered with by the arrival of this man with fresh evidence – or else the murder was committed from utter despair, by a prisoner who had no hope of release and who was determined to end the life of the man who had been responsible for his present plight. So, I was looking for a name at the top of the board, or else one at the very bottom.

Certainly, C7 and W9 were nearing the top of the scoreboard and might be brought forward for early release quite soon if they kept up their progress. Any man who caused them to lose some hard-earned marks might be in danger from a convict desperate to escape the prison ship and its dreary and cruel life, I thought, as I winced at the sound of a whip, followed by the scream of a man in acute pain. The warder had left the deck and no doubt came across a prisoner infringing one of the ship's laws. I tried not to think of the pain that had been inflicted for some minor misdeed and concentrated on looking for clues.

The two men at the top of the board were worth thinking about if I could find any link between them and the dead man. And then there were the names on the bottom of the board – convicts who had nothing to lose and who might be full of resentment and anger towards a man who may have been responsible for an unjust sentence which confined him to this living hell.

I looked around. There was no still no sign of the warder, but another man with a whip in his hand came across the deck and dipped the thong of his whip into the river water.

I shuddered slightly at the thought that he was washing off
the blood of some unfortunate convict from the thong, but I
suppressed my aversion and approached him in as friendly a
fashion as I could manage.

'Terrible business, the murder of that gentleman,' I said
with a jerk of my head towards the place where the body of
the dead man was being transferred to a cart by some of the
policemen.

'Yes, indeed, sir,' he said politely. 'There will be a lot of
trouble until the police decide on who did it. Still, if it was
one of our lads, we'll soon get a confession out of them,' he
added in an offhand manner and lifting his whip from the river
water, he cracked it a couple of times – perhaps to dissipate
the river water, but it sounded in the air like a threat.

I shuddered slightly at the sound. I almost expected to hear
a scream to follow it. I wondered how many false confessions
were extracted by the brutality of that whip.

'Might have been one of Mr Dickens' guests,' I said and
watched his face.

He looked amused, I thought.

'One of the ladies or gentlemen, sir, are you serious?' he
asked in an incredulous fashion and then shook his head with
a half-smile upon his face.

'The police are going to question Mr Dickens' guests as
soon as they get back to Gad's Hill House,' I informed him,
and his smile grew broader.

'Is that a fact, sir?' he said politely. 'Well, well, well! We'll
see.'

'Do you think it unlikely to be one of the guests?' I asked
the question, although the answer was known to me.

He didn't bother replying, just raised his face to the sky.
'More snow in the air, sir,' he commented and then abandoned
me with a polite nod just as the warder returned full of apolo-
gies for leaving me unattended.

'Let me find someone who will show you around the ship,
now, in case the two policemen decide to go back early,' he
said. 'They probably won't take too long. In fact, they may
be ready for me, by now, so I'll say goodbye now, sir and
hand you over to one of my trusty men.'

He put a whistle to his lips and blew three short blasts and
then waited. I was going to be handed over to number three,
I guessed, and made a mental note about the whistle just in
case I did write that book. I wondered how dangerous it was
to work on one of those prison ships. And how important
was it to have an agreed means of summoning aid – something like that whistle would carry easily in the open air. The
man, presumably number three, arrived very briskly.

'Nearly through, now, sir,' he said to the warder who
queried him with just a lift of the eyebrows. 'Got all the names
and numbers, sir,' he continued. 'Police found six suspects,
sir.'

I was intrigued by that. How did the police decide so
quickly on suspects from among the men whom they were
questioning?

'But the dead man, Mr Timmy O'Connor, wouldn't have
been known to any of your convicts, would he?' I asked with
as much an air of surprise as I could produce. 'Surely they
wouldn't have any reason to murder him, would they?'

'They might have seen him in court,' replied the warder.
'He owned this ship, you know, and gentlemen who invest
in ships do attend court hearings to make sure that they get
a conviction. No point in owning a prison ship unless you
keep it full of convicts, sir. No money, no income, just all
expenses unless the ship is kept as full as possible. That
poor gentleman who has just been killed was very good at
keeping the numbers up in his ship. There were times during
the last few years when I've been working here that I'd have
found it hard to fit an extra fly on board. A great man he
was! Paid our wages on time, with an extra bonus for
reporting bad behaviour. Bad behaviour always lengthens
the sentence, you see, sir.'

I began to feel a bit sickened. Originally, I had been hoping
that one of the convicts would have been found guilty, but
now that I had witnessed the brutality with which these unfortunate men were treated, I began to feel that I would do
anything to have the police find a culprit among Dickens'
guests. Dickens' guests would all have the means to employ
a good lawyer to defend them. A good lawyer would probably

dissuade the police from an accusation and if that did not work, and if the matter came to a court case, a good lawyer would have an excellent chance of obtaining a 'not guilty' verdict due to the lack of evidence and after a while the whole matter would be allowed to die down and be registered as an unsolved case.

But once the police focused upon the convicts, there was no doubt in my mind that evidence, and a confession, would be brutally beaten out of one of these unfortunate fellows. The thought sickened me, and I made up my mind to find a possible culprit, or better still, a number of possible culprits from among the Christmas guests and give the police the task of sifting through the evidence. With a bit of luck, that could take many months. If a man was guilty, it was only right that he should hang. But this should only happen once all possibilities had been carefully gone through and there should be no chance that a confession was extracted by fear of the whip. I shuddered again and decided that if faced with that whip I might well decide that life was not worth living and I would make a false confession, having decided that hanging was better than the agony of a flagellation.

My task, I told myself, was to discover the truth and then I, as a private citizen, unlike a policeman, could decide what to do with my evidence. In the meantime, I must make use of the lucky chance which gave me access to these men who were working in the River Medway estuary and on the banks near to the little church and graveyard, near to the place where the victim had been killed.

'I wonder,' I said to the warder, 'whether I would be allowed to have a chat with those men who were working today on the river below the graveyard. Would it be possible to identify which men they were?'

I hoped that some record would be kept as I guessed that none of these unfortunate convicts would voluntarily confess to working near to the place where the gentleman was killed. They would all be too afraid that they would be savagely beaten to extract a confession.

'You're in luck, there, sir,' said the warder. 'I myself was supervising a group just down there below the churchyard.

The men were digging, just digging out the sandy soil and piling it up. I like to wait until we have had a good go at the digging when they're fresh, before I let them slacken off and fill the buckets. They work better at the hard stuff when they're fresh and they go faster because they know that when twenty buckets are filled then I'll let them have a break just carrying the stuff up and then dumping it.'

I glowed with excitement. This man seemed an intelligent fellow and even if I didn't get much from the convicts, I might get some good evidence from him.

'No threats of the whip, now,' I said to him earnestly. 'I want these men to tell me what happened, not to make up something that they think will please me.'

He looked at me with surprise and even some amusement, but made no comment, other than the usual, 'Yes, sir.'

'Do you think that you will be able to remember which men were with you this afternoon?' I asked. The convicts, each one of them with a shaven head and wearing identical suits of clothing, looked to me as alike as a herd of brown cows on the marshes.

In answer, he put his whistle to his lips and blew six double notes from it. Within a couple of minutes there was the rhythmic sound of marching feet and the now familiar note of the crack of a whip. Twelve prisoners, dressed in identical uniforms, all with shaven heads, came trotting onto the deck just like a batch of well-trained dogs. They came to a stand-still in front of the warder, standing in a straight line, hands clasped in front of them, and eyes fixed upon the whip in the man's hand.

'These were the men working on that side of the hillside, sir,' said the warder.

'I see,' I said. I wondered whether there was any way of getting rid of the warder and having a friendly conversation with the prisoners, but there was something about the dead expression in the eyes of each one of them that made me regard them as less than human. And, to be honest, I wasn't sure whether I was brave enough to be left alone with these men. They looked strong and muscular – any one of them, I guessed, would be able to pick me up and throw me into the sea in a couple of seconds. And if that happened, doubtless all would swear to ignorance about what had happened. No, I desperately needed the presence and the co-operation of the warder.

I would pick them out, one by one, I decided, and I would pose a question for each. I pointed to the middle of the line, to a man with a scar across his cheekbone.

'You there, man with a scar on your cheek, a question for you. How far up the hill did you empty the buckets?'

He said nothing, just looked from under his eyelashes at the man who stood beside him.

I tried again. 'Did you get up as far as the burial ground wall?'

That was a direct question which he could not duck.

'No, sir.'

Information – not of any use, but information. I smiled approval and gratitude.

'Good man. That's what I want. A man who remembers things. Like tobacco?' I asked and when he nodded, I took a stick of tobacco from a pouch within my pocket and handed it to him. With a glance at the warder, he began to chew the tobacco like one who is desperate for an almost forgotten taste. Every head was turned towards him.

'Another question. Hands up, anyone who can answer it. See anyone, see any stranger – someone not from your ship?' I asked and saw the faces brighten. Every hand was raised. I had asked the wrong question; a simple 'yes' would be an easy answer, I told myself. So, I added, 'I need to know who they were. You won't have a name, but you can tell me what they looked like; what they were wearing.' I kept my eyes upon them and avoided looking at the warder. He might be a more reliable witness, but I could interrogate him later. I thought it was more likely, though, that a convict would see someone lurking at the top of the hill. The warder's eyes would be on the convicts to make sure that none of them could escape, as, though they were, of course, shackled, it still would be possible for a determined man to get away from the group and hide somewhere – perhaps not be missed. No, I decided, the warders' attention would have been on the prisoners and so my best chance was that a bored and exhausted convict would take a break from the heavy work of carrying buckets of sodden sand and mud and would stand for a moment surveying the marshes, the little churchyard, and its poignant graveyard.

'I'll need a good description, appearance and clothing, or you are of no use to me,' I repeated and noticed, without surprise, that many hands began to go down as the convicts eyed one another suspiciously. The warder stirred uneasily, and I began to realize that I might be about to cause trouble. The warder had a slightly worried air and I told myself that the atmosphere on these prison ships was that of a fire about to explode. There must be about a couple of hundred men staring at me. Far too many for a universal distribution of tobacco to chew. I hesitated and looked at the warder. His mouth was compressed, and he gave a slight shake of his head. I was quick to take the hint.

'Anyone see a man with one leg, up on the hillside,' I asked with an innocent air and every hand went up instantly. I laughed.

'I'll have to go away and rob a tobacco shop of a couple of hundred sticks of tobacco, and then I'll be back,' I said lightly, shook my head at the warder and stood back to allow him and his assistant to manage the situation. There was a lot of shouting and I winced at the cracking of whips but hoped that these vicious blows had not landed upon human flesh. I decided that I would beg in the streets rather than do a job like that warder but waited in expectation that he might have some information for me.

He was back remarkably quickly and with him was one of the convicts, limping along with his shackled legs. How could these unfortunate men live like that, shackled and beaten. I decided that I would throw myself into the waters of the Medway river rather than endure the life and wondered how many convicts were lost through suicide. And then I thought about the death of a man who owned a convict ship. If I were a convict, I thought, I would take a chance upon death by hanging to avenge myself. Hanging would be a quick and easy death compared to the living torture that these poor men endured.

And then I thought about my own role in this. Any hint to the police that the murder could have been committed by a convict would immediately spur the warders to an effort to get the truth through the usual methods – the torture of the whip and a deprivation of food and even water on occasion.

I would, I decided, deflect the police into the examination of the fellow guests of the dead man. All of these were well-to-do persons who would be treated with respect by the police. The dead man's nephews, of course, had to come under suspicion, and certainly each of the three nephews: Swayne, Bypers and Caleb, would be prime suspects. But there were, I told myself, three of them – three who always seemed to stay together, three who each had equal reason to be angry with their uncle who had cheated them out of their inheritance. The police could be kept busy weighing up the motives. And then there were those of Dickens' guests who had, perhaps, been victims of the extortions of a man who ran a moneylending business and who had cheated and despoiled them. These had all been present when the man was killed. But surely all of these could afford a good solicitor who would make sure that the police could see that the evidence was too nebulous for conviction. And if anyone, like poor Georgina, did not have the money for legal aid, I was sure that both I and Dickens would come to the rescue. And then I thought of someone else . . .

The thought of that person flashed through my mind as the convict limped towards me. I turned a welcoming face towards him and nodded my thanks to the warder who, rather grim-faced, kept a left hand on one of the man's shackled wrists and who, from time to time, flourished the whip in his own right hand.

'Yes, my good man,' I said to the convict and noticed that he seemed rather surprised and quite tongue-tied at my choice of words. Had anyone ever called him 'good' before now? I felt a wave of pity for him and hoped that I would be able to justify, in the warder's eyes, giving a cigarette to the poor fellow.

'I saw someone come out of the church, sir,' said the convict and then added, 'two people, arm in arm. A lady and a gentleman, sir.'

That did not sound so hopeful. A lady and gentleman, arm in arm, were unlikely to roll a heavy statue down the hill to smash into pieces a man who was lying there, lost in a drunken sleep. Nevertheless, any information could lead on to further discoveries and so I nodded encouragingly.

'Go on,' I said. 'What did they look like?'

He described the lady first and I had a moment's pity for him when I realized how detailed the description was; this poor man would be deprived of female society – neither mother, sister, nor wife, nor daughter. No visitors were allowed on to these convict ships. He had observed her so closely, remembered what she had been wearing, remembered the colour of her hair and how tall she was. It was, in fact, a perfect description of my friend, Georgina. I knew a moment's disappointment, though, as he went on to describe the gentleman with her. Not for one minute would I ever have suspected my poor friend, Jas, and I didn't think that the police were likely to suspect him, either.

Now that I knew that Georgina and Jas had been outside the church, I could have a word with one of them – Jas, initially, for preference, as he would be the more reliable, but I would not neglect to question Georgina also, and there was a remote possibility that one or the other may have spotted someone else. Ideally, I thought, with a grimace, I would like to find evidence that a bunch of people, the more the better, had had the opportunity of tipping over that statue and setting it rolling down the hill to strike the sleeping man. If the police had five or better still, six suspects from amongst Dickens' guests, then, including the three nephews of the dead man, that would be about ten suspects, all hopefully, in the eyes of the police bearing a grudge against the dead man, Timmy O'Connor.

Ten suspects would keep the police very busy and, I hoped, so confuse the issue that eventually the enquiry would peter out and the case would be shelved among the unsolved murders.

And, I reckoned, no one would care if that happened. There

would be no pressure put upon the police once the newspapers lost interest in the affair. As far as I knew, only the four wronged nephews were left of the immediate family. They would, I was sure, have no sorrow about the killing of their uncle who had deprived them of money which should have been theirs. They would, I was quite sure, make no fuss about looking for the man, or woman, who did the deed. They would divide, amongst themselves, the fortune that the dead man had probably accumulated, including, of course, the money he had recently inherited from the aunt in London. I could not imagine them putting pressure on the police to solve the murder of a man who had cheated them and whose death had now benefited them.

I took out my notebook and made a note of all that I had learned from the convicts. I might refer to it, but I would be careful with that information. There would be no question of handing over the spoken words to the police, or of giving the police the name or the number of the men who had spoken to me. There was, I decided to say, no real reason to suspect any of the convicts. They were closely supervised, and they were always in a pair so that any murder would have had to be devised between two people – a dangerous affair and a warder was always present whenever I had seen convicts working. It would, I guessed, have been impossible for a convict to be alone, unshackled and unsupervised in any way.

And so, I thanked the warder and he beckoned to a man to row me back to the sands again.

# TEN

By the time that the police wagon dropped me off at Gad's Hill, all the windows of the house were lit up and the rest of Dickens' guests had already changed out of their damp clothes and muddy boots. Gathered around a blazing fire in the library, all were happily quaffing some restoring glassfuls of spirits. There was no sign of the nephews of the dead man. They had probably, sensing the awkwardness of their situation, or needing to talk over what to do now, stayed in their room and allowed Dickens' guests the freedom to discuss the exciting affair of the murder of their uncle without any restraint which their presence may have induced.

Spirits, I sensed, were high and the atmosphere was that of excitement. There was an ironic cheer when I came into the room.

'Well done, Wilkie,' said Jas. 'I see you have escaped police custody, my friend. Tell us how you did it!'

'Don't tease him,' said Georgina, putting a protective arm on my shoulders. 'I was the prime suspect until they seized upon poor Wilkie. I shall be eternally grateful to him. They say that you were taken on board the prison ship, Wilkie. Were you put in irons? How did you escape?'

I nestled a little closer to Georgina. She did smell deliciously scented and I was happy to see the jealousy in most men's eyes.

'Tell you later,' I said in a loud stage whisper, theatrically shielding my mouth with my hand. I noticed that the nephews of the dead man quietly entered the room but they retired to the bookshelves by the door.

'But in the meantime, she can tell us something now,' said Jas. 'Why were you prime suspect, my darling? Do tell!'

I could feel the tension in the woman's body so close to mine, could hear her sharply suck in a breath of air, then see

her compressed lips and the widened eyes and I knew that I
had to do something to shield Georgina.

'She was protecting someone,' I said with an air of mock
solemnity. I looked around at the faces, some puzzled, others
amused, none, I felt, taking me seriously.

'Protecting whom?'

'*She* says that you were protecting her!' exclaimed John
Forster.

'Tell us the truth, Wilkie. Go on, tell us. Are you the true
suspect, Wilkie?'

'Is she a witness or a suspect?'

It was as I had hoped. The questions came fast, but the
atmosphere was jocose and frivolous.

'Sit down, everyone,' I said. I released Georgina and made
my way towards the fire. Its heat was welcome after the cold
outside, but I chose the place, standing within the fireplace,
with one hand resting upon the mantelpiece, knowing that now
I was a natural focus for the eyes of the assembled guests.
Every face was visible to me, some were sitting upon chairs,
many on the padded arms of the easy chairs, others piled upon
couches and every face of Dickens' guests was illuminated by
the firelight as well as by the candles. Dickens, himself, I saw,
had withdrawn into the shadow of a large bookcase, but that
did not matter. I would have plenty of opportunities to share
my ideas with him and to gauge his reactions. Now was the
time when I could concentrate upon the guests, many of whom
were barely known to me. Was one of them guilty of the
murder of the moneylender?

'Once upon a time,' I began, using the time-honoured
formula to give me a moment to think. 'Once upon a time,' I
repeated, 'there was a man, a wicked man who made money
from the misery . . .' This was getting a little too abrupt, too
near to the truth, so I hastily deviated as I did not wish to
involve the victims in my story. 'Well, this man, this wicked
man caused great anger and great anxiety to many people. He
delved into past lives and paid money for information about
those who were rich and famous. And, little by little, he accumulated dangerous pieces of knowledge . . .' I paused there
for a moment. There was a reaction in the room – difficult to

say from where, but I sensed a tension from my audience. I turned, threw a log upon the fire, and then turned back to my audience.

'Men went to prison on his evidence,' I said, slowly and carefully, leaving a few seconds to elapse until I continued. 'Many men went to prison, my friends, and others were sent by the courts out as convicts to Australia because of secrets which this man had uncovered. They, both the prisoners and the convicts, were the ones who could not find money to pay him to keep their secrets. But many, especially when they saw what happened to others, did pay him for his silence and these lived lives of anxiety and poverty, all the time fearing that more than they could afford would be demanded from them and that, ultimately, he would ruin and disgrace them. In the meantime, he grew rich and powerful and purchased . . .' I allowed a pause here and then finished my sentence. 'He purchased prison ships,' I said. Again I stopped. My last words had drawn a sharp intake of breath from someone, but I was not sure from whom the sound had come. I had to proceed, and so I finished my tale.

'Yes, indeed,' I said, 'this wicked man purchased some of those so-called prison ships, ships that were used as floating prisons, ships which enabled him to make money from the incarceration of those whose secrets he had already discovered and of those who still held secrets to be discovered. From time to time, ladies and gentlemen, this rich and powerful man visited the prison ships that he owned and under the pretext of helping the convicts to prepare for a new life after their prison sentence had ended, he delved into the history of these prisoners . . .' I left a silence for a moment, noting with satisfaction that all eyes were fixed upon me. There was, I thought, a measure of bewilderment in all faces except the faces of the three Irishmen, the nephews of the dead man. They turned impassive countenances towards me. My revelations were not new to them. They were aware of the history of their uncle; they knew of his investments.

'Crimes rarely involve one person only, ladies and gentlemen,' I went on. 'This man who wanted to be rich and powerful soon began to accumulate a store of knowledge about the underworld in the great city of London. He found a name, investigated a crime, found a connection with another crime and then another name and another name, until a whole network of criminals and dastardly deeds were exposed to him. The more he found out, the more new knowledge that was exposed to him and the more knowledge he acquired of the underworld, the more money he acquired through blackmail and bribery, or else provided fodder for his prison ships. Matters went on like this for . . .'

I stopped. A door had opened at the back of the room, just barely wide enough for three men to leave the room, to slide through the half-opened door, one after the other. And then the door was shut so quietly and carefully that not even the noise of a click was to be heard in the room. The three nephews of the dead man were gone from the room – out of embarrassment, maybe, or perhaps to talk over the matter.

During that short time of silence, I, once again, allowed my eyes to wander over the company and to note the different expressions on the faces of Dickens' friends. Georgina had moved a few steps away from me, keeping her head averted and turned so close to the fire that her cheeks were bright red. I turned my attention to three of Dickens' guests I barely knew: young Danson passed his fingers across his fledgling moustache and then began to crunch savagely upon the last nail of his left-hand fingers; Mayhew stiffened perceptibly; and the eyes of Bertrand Chapman – one of Dickens' publishers – widened with concern as he looked from me to Dickens and then back upon his nephew, Jonathan's worried face.

There was no doubt in my mind that the murder of this man, this moneylender, had affected many of the guests attending this pleasant Christmas gathering in Dickens' hospitable house. It may have occasioned little sorrow, but clearly had caused much anxiety. I felt satisfied, even slightly thrilled at the reaction which I had aroused. I lowered my voice almost to a whisper and finished my story. 'For many years,' I continued, 'he led that life, until one day, one cold and snowy day, he met his nemesis. There was a man, a man who was a famous novelist, and this man knew that something was going on, that friends, acquaintances, friends of friends, were having their lives turned into days and nights of misery. This novelist engaged a lady of fashion to work for him and between them both . . .' I broke off here and allowed my gaze to wander along the line of guests but avoided Dickens' penetrating stare, before continuing. 'Between them both, they chanced upon a person, a name, a possibility, and then an almost certainty . . .' I looked around the room again; each pair of eyes, including Georgina's, was wide with curiosity – Dickens' eyes, which he had narrowed to focus more intently upon my face. In Dickens' mind, there was only one famous novelist in the room, himself, of course, and he wondered, I knew, what I was going to reveal.

I looked away hastily from him and continued my story.

'And the lady of fashion brought her wiles to work upon this person, this name, this possibility . . . this possibility which had now turned into an almost certainty. And when she induced him to walk with her across a deserted marshland, well . . .' I stopped. Every face was still turned towards me, every eye was focused upon me and there was a dead silence in the room.

'Well . . . well . . . what?' Leech, the illustrator of Dickens' books, was the one who eventually broke the silence.

I shrugged my shoulders. Now was the moment for the comic conclusion.

'Don't know,' I said in an offhand fashion. 'I haven't made up that part of the story yet. It should make a great play in the West End. I need to make up a good character for the famous novelist, find a top-class actor for that part and another top-class actress for the lady friend, of course. I must talk to Macready when next I see him, when I manage to get the time to.' I waved my hands about, while still observing faces as closely as I could.

Another long silence, a silence while Dickens' friends looked furtively one at the other and then across at Dickens himself.

A few seconds of silence! Rather a revealing silence, I thought, as I scanned the faces. Even Georgina looked at me with tightened mouth and horror-filled eyes. No one laughed – nobody even smiled.

I waited for a few moments and then said slowly, 'I suppose that it ended in a death. The only possible ending, don't you agree, my friends?'

Still the silence, but this time it was short-lived. Dickens was on his feet, clapping enthusiastically and after that short silence others began to join in. As always happened, where Dickens led, others followed!

There was, oddly enough, an atmosphere of relief in the room. Smiles on faces. Backs stretched, heads turned, conversations begun, light, gossipy conversations. No one spoke of murder – not that I could hear.

Dickens, now with a carefree, smiling face, touched a bell and within seconds plates festooned with piping hot mince pies were carried in by one servant and a trayful of glasses by another. Dickens, along with Frank and Walter, hastened to produce bottles of sherry and brandy, and then Kate Dickens came with the hot Gin Punch and her eldest daughter, Mamie, carried Dickens' favourite Smoking Bishop, a concoction of mulled wine and citrus punch mixed with port.

I took the liberty of securing two glasses, one of the Smoking Bishop and the other of Gin Punch and then made my way over to Georgina. 'Take your pick,' I said loudly and clearly and then, with a furtive glance over my shoulder, I moved a little closer to her.

'What did you think of my little story?' I asked in a low tone.

She looked at me and oddly I could swear that there was a frightened look in her eyes. Surely, she was not taking it seriously! I began to be sorry that I had tried to be funny. I never dreamt that she would be frightened by my nonsense.

'The Gin Punch, please,' she said in a clear and slightly raised voice and when I had handed it to her, she turned away from me, deliberately turning a cold shoulder to me, and began talking to John Forster instead. Even though I moved away, I overheard a couple of phrases and one of them stung me – 'You know what Collins is like,' she said. 'Always exaggerates. You can't trust a word that he says. He shows off, looking for attention.'

I did, I suppose, have a reputation for tall tales, and so it

was not that which upset me, so much. No, it was her use of
the word 'Collins'. Why had she called me that? We had been
friends for years – had been on first name terms for years.
Why should she suddenly call me 'Collins' in that contemp-
tuous and dismissive way? And why give the impression that
I told lies, when she knew quite well that I did not. I might
exaggerate, but that was for fun. I did not deliberately set out
to deceive my friends. Had I been stupid? Had I betrayed her
confidence? Should I have been more cautious? I looked around
the room, but Dickens had hoisted one of his sons upon his
shoulders and was declaiming loudly that he needed a lawyer.
He caught my eye and smiled upon me.

'Collins,' he said. 'Come and help me. You, after your years
of study, must be the nearest thing to a lawyer in this room.
This little fellow has given me so many excellent reasons as
to why he should not go to bed that, Lord preserve me, I need
a lawyer to restore my authority!'

Thankfully I hastened over to him. As theatrically as I could,
I produced a watch and invited Henry to state as many reasons
as he possibly could within the space of just one minute. This
attracted attention and the guests crowded around our three
figures and displayed smiling faces as they looked upon the
little boy, perched on his father's shoulder, looking very pleased
with himself as his younger brother, Plorn, and guest, Carrie,
were already in bed.

'Go on, Henry' I said encouragingly. 'Start talking! Keep
talking! I'll do the timing.'

Henry, I had often thought, was the cleverest of Dickens'
sons. Any other child when confronted with a sea of guests
would have put a finger in his mouth and turned silent, averting
his gaze from the faces just below his own. But not young
Henry! It was amazing how fluent the little fellow was, and
how many reasons he produced, starting with the ordinary
arguments and progressing to rather adult-sounding sentences,
probably overheard from his father, It was, he declared, very
bad for a child's nerves to have a guest of his father's murdered
and it would be quite understandable that a sensitive child like
himself would sleep badly, What I need,' he told the amused
audience, 'is to be tired, exhausted, weary, fatigued, drowsy

. . .' Hardly stopping to draw breath, the little fellow produced so many synonyms for 'tired' that the guests began to clap, even giving their own suggestions in loud whispers that stimulated him into his final flourish. 'And, so dear Papa,' he said, 'unless thoroughly tired and dropping asleep from exhaustion, I shall be condemned to lie awake all night with my mind spinning around, endeavouring to prove your innocence of the deed of murder. I think that I need to go and help in the kitchen for a half hour or so before going to bed – purely, dearest Papa, to clear the young mind of your beloved son of anxiety.'

There was, I noticed, a slight silence after these closing words, and a shade of embarrassment seemed to cross the faces of the visitors as they stole glances at Dickens' face. Why had the child thought that his father might be guilty of murder? Had it been a joke uttered in fun by one of his elder brothers who would have been horrified to witness the awkward silence that resulted from the child's words?

But Bertrand Chapman, always the soul of tact, broke the silence with a loud and energetic clap which resounded through the numerous lampshades.

'Bravo, son of Dickens!' he declared. 'Bravo young Dickenson! That boy is a master of words. Takes after his father. I do declare that Henry should be permitted another twenty minutes helping in the kitchen to clear his mind – and the plates, of course – of anxiety and prepare him for sleep. Those in favour, shout "aye".'

Of course, everyone shouted 'aye' and Dickens bore off young Henry, sitting triumphantly upon his shoulders, in the direction of the kitchen while the rest of the guests, to my secret amusement, began animatedly to discuss the murder in quite a relaxed and unembarrassed fashion. The consensus of opinions was, of course, that one of the convicts murdered him and I joined in happily, telling everyone about the purchase of the convict ship by the dead man; a ship which, of course, I insisted should be called a 'hulk', anyone who called it a ship had to pay a shilling in forfeit – I promising that the forfeit money should be used to buy cigarettes for the convicts.

And when I had related all I knew about the history of the hulks, I began telling them about the interest in the dead man from the convict who was my informant. I made a good story out of it and soon I found myself in the centre of the group, revelling in my newfound popularity until I noticed that Georgina, looking white-faced and heavy-eyed, seemed to be drinking heavily. Not like her, I thought, and I wondered why she appeared to be so upset by the death of a man who had persecuted her and, according to herself, had made her life into a burden. I would, I thought, have a word with her, taking the opportunity of my temporary popularity.

Full of curiosity, I broke off, waving my hands in the air and I mimed a sore throat by clutching my neck and then crossing over to the sideboard where one of Dickens' friendly servants smiled indulgently at me and poured out a generous glass of sherry. I drank it, sip by sip, until my audience grew tired of waiting for any more details and went over to listen to one of Dickens' stories about a marvellously strange old, white-haired woman, glimpsed behind a window in Rochester, who, he fancied, would make a wonderful basis for an exciting new novel that he was planning. Despite the prestigious amount of energy which he was expending upon his guests and upon creating a memorable and a marvellous Christmas for his large family of children, I could see by his absorbed expression that Dickens was now in the throes of composing a story. Doubtless the strange, bleak marshland, the small church, the burial ground with the stone statues of dead children, all of these would come together to form the background to one of his exciting stories. And the glimpse of the strange woman with the white hair, as described by him, may have been the trigger that every author needs before plunging into work.

I looked at him affectionately. My dear friend, Charles Dickens! A character larger than life. I had been tempted to hint to him about Georgina's problems, to ask advice for her, to discuss the strange death of the man whom I still thought of as Uncle Timmy, but then I changed my mind. Dickens, I thought, had enough to deal with. One of his guests had been murdered and it would be for him to arrange all the formalities. The three nephews of the dead man had not yet appeared, but he would have to make sure that all was well with them, he would, I was sure, take it upon himself to help them in dealing with the police. And he would probably have to organize matters for them by making all of those complicated arrangements for the removal of the dead man from Kent in England, back to southern Ireland, once, of course, the police had released the body.

And, of course, as well as matters dealing with the murdered man and his nephews, Dickens had his other guests to think about. He, after all, was the host; and a superb host, I told myself with an affectionate smile tugging at my lips. His wife, Kate, was an amiable woman, but it was Dickens, himself, who saw to the children's Christmas presents, encouraged them in their plans to put on a yearly play, and made all the arrangements. He made sure that all his guests had an enjoyable Christmas, he arranged suitable food for all – I had seen him in many an earnest conference with the cook – and he was the one who checked that the bedrooms were comfortable and well-stocked with everything that was needed to make it a memorable few days for his guests. He organized the entertainments, made sure that everyone was included and was enjoying themselves, and now, of course, he had to deal with the police about the murder of one of his guests while still determinedly maintaining the Christmas atmosphere. Nothing from carol singing to traditional Christmas parlour games to the best of food and of drink would be found lacking from the Dickens Christmas festival.

The least that I could do to help him was to assemble as many facts about the dead man as possible and then share my knowledge with him and if he thought it was the right thing to do, to share it with the police. In the meantime, I would try to find out what was wrong with Georgina and help her to sort out a plausible story before she was interviewed by the police. I would, I thought, be tactful about this, would not embarrass her, just be available if she needed help. With a quick glance around the room, I moved quietly away from the noisy crowd who were swapping ideas at the top of their voices and edged my way to where she stood beside the window.

I waited quietly by Georgina's side, both of us standing, shoulder to shoulder and staring through the window where a few flakes of snow drifted harmlessly through the air and settled upon hedges and shrub tops. Her eyes were fixed on the wintery scene and she did not look at me.

'What's the matter?' I said quietly.

'Nothing's the matter.' Her voice was harsh and a little higher than usual. I saw a few heads turn in her direction and then turn away again in a slightly embarrassed way. Georgina, I thought, was attracting attention and that was stupid. Dickens, as usual, had a mixed crowd of visitors – some were the nicest, kindest men and women in London, but others were gossips who loved a tale that they could spread through a wide bunch of acquaintances. If Georgina were not more careful, she could find her affairs whispered about all over London, or at least amongst circles of friends and acquaintances.

'The police are taking a great interest in the convicts, poor devils. But, of course,' I added in as casual a manner as I could devise, 'they will want to get a statement from each and *every* single *one* of us.' I emphasized my words to make sure she understood my meaning. 'I've just been devising my statement. I'll have to have a word with Dickens and make sure that our accounts tally. He can be my alibi and I can be his, as both of us spent what must have been the time of the murder together. What about you? What are you going to say, Georgina?'

I had, I thought, sounded as casual as possible, but I could see her stiffen.

'How should I have been involved? What are you insinuating?' Her voice was aggressive and challenging. I, in my turn, stiffened. I was getting tired of Georgina. Why was she suddenly so hostile to me? After all, I was doing everything possible to be a help to her. Surely her own common sense would tell her that the police would find out the occupation of the dead man and would swiftly move to find out if any one of his clients who had borrowed money from his firm were amongst the guests at Gad's Hill and had taken part in that walk to Cooling graveyard.

Still, she was an old friend and now a girl in trouble. With an effort I bit back my annoyance and answered her question as gently as possible. 'I'm afraid, Georgina, that anyone who had borrowed money from that unpleasant man and who was present there at that church or in the churchyard this morning will, inevitably, come under suspicion.'

'Perhaps someone who, like you, deliberately arranged an alibi, would fall under more suspicion,' she snapped.

I couldn't believe my ears. What on earth did she mean? How could I be said to have arranged an alibi?

'My dear Georgina,' I said patiently. 'Neither I nor Dickens, I am quite sure, had the slightest necessity to borrow money, so I don't think that we will fall under suspicion.'

I left her, then. I was feeling quite hurt. How could she accuse me, and Dickens, of fabricating an alibi? She herself had pointed out that I was well-off because of the money left by my late father, and Dickens, the whole world knew, had sold millions of copies of his latest book, *A Tale of Two Cities*. Yes, he had a big family, but so long as he could write books which the world was eager to read, why then money would pour into his bank account. I was reasonably sure of that fact.

Nevertheless, her words had left me feeling a little uneasy. The sooner this mystery of the marshland murder was cleared up, the more at ease we would all be. Surely it should be easy to find a number of people who should be investigated by the police and who should provide enough clues to keep the police busy until the real murderer was pinpointed. It was, after all, I told myself, quite a simple problem. Apart from the convicts and the guards, all who were present on that afternoon on the marshland were known to me and so I should be able to work out whether any one of those men or women had a hand in the murder of this unpleasant man.

If only I knew a little more about him and his background. I was reluctant to cross-question Georgina any further, but there seemed no other way to glean information about someone who held the disreputable occupation of a moneylender. None of Dickens' visitors would be happy to be expansive about a moneylender – or even, in fact, to acknowledge anything but the most superficial of relationships.

And then I remembered something else. *Aroo from Cork; I am, aroo?* A smile came to my lips as I murmured the doggerel.

I would slip out of the room, unnoticed amongst the noisy crowd and I would visit Pat in the stables. My excuse would be acceptable. His employer, Dickens, was busy with police and visitors and I came, in his place, to tell Pat what was happening.

Surely, in the case of a murder, any man would be intensely curious and anxious to find out what was happening. We had all rather overlooked Pat in the excitement; had burdened him with the care of women and children on his cart. I would, I thought, be a welcome visitor to the stables as he was bound to want to discuss the dramatic moment when the corpse was discovered and surely he would be able to glean some useful information about his fellow Cork citizen. With a quick glance around and a mutter to Jas, I left the room.

As I had thought, Pat was pleased to see me. I had no sooner enquired from one of the stable lads about his whereabouts, when the man himself came to the door.

'Well, Mr Collins, come for a ride on your favourite pony?' he asked in a humorous fashion, as he hung a lantern to a hook outside the door.

I did not hesitate to take up the joke. 'I don't think that he likes me too much,' I said. 'In fact, I think he prefers to go for a run on his own. If I remember rightly, the last time we met, he was over the hills before I finished buttoning my jacket.'

'Well, let's walk over and you can say hello to him. I'll introduce you so that he knows you mean no harm. You lads get those stables cleaned out while I go across to the ten-acre field with Mr Collins.'

That was neatly done, I thought and felt a ray of hope that Pat had something of interest to tell me.

'What a day!' I said as we went through the gate.

'You can say that again.' There was a relieved and enthusiastic note in his voice which showed me that he was pleased that I had opened the conversation.

'You saw the body, didn't you, Pat?' I asked and he nodded.

'God almighty! What a sight! Right mess he was and that's for sure!' he said cheerfully, and I realized that we did not need to waste time with any false prayers or regrets for the dead man.

'You knew all about him, didn't you?' I said, giving a perfunctory glance at the horse and then looking swiftly away to assure him that I had no plans for riding him.

This piece of by-play brought a smile to his face, and the atmosphere relaxed even more.

'I did, to be sure,' said Pat with an emphatic note in his voice.

I took a chance. 'Nothing good to be known about that fellow, I'd say, was there?' I asked in a nonchalant way, while, hopefully, assuring him that I was no friend to the murdered man.

He gave me a sideways look. 'You wouldn't be trying to get me into trouble, Mr Collins,' he said.

I held up my two hands with both middle fingers bent over the forefingers to make something of a criss-cross shape.

'Cross my heart and hope to die,' I said.

'Sure, we'll make a holy priest out of you one of these days!' he said in the easy-going way that the Irish seemed to talk about religion.

To my pleasure, Pat sounded quite relaxed, and I ventured to push the conversation onto the next stage.

'Well, I haven't heard anything good about him from the people around here. It would have been the same over in Cork. Would I be right?' I queried.

'You would indeed,' he said, nodding his head to add emphasis to his words, and I relaxed. The man's confidence had been won.

'Trouble is that a man like that makes enemies of the nicest of people,' he said in an offhand manner.

'You'd be right about that,' I said with a nod and noticed that a trace of an Irish accent seemed to be creeping into my own voice. 'Got a lot of surprising people under his thumb over here in England. You could have cut the atmosphere with a knife when he appeared at the dinner table last night. Was he up to the same tricks back there in Cork?' I added in a careless fashion.

'You can say that again,' he said.

'Cheated you, did he?' I suggested and he gave me a sour smile and half shook his head.

'Ah, you saw him coming,' I said with a congratulatory nod.

'Heard stories,' was his reply and he delivered it with an effort at preserving the smile, but I noticed how his face had darkened. 'To tell you the truth . . .' He began a sentence and then shrugged his shoulders and stared morosely ahead.

'Moneylending, was that it? Moneylending and cheating – that's what he seemed to be up to, over here,' I suggested and watched his face.

He shrugged. 'Moneylending is a business like any other, I suppose,' he said. 'My old father used to say to us boys, "Neither a lender nor a borrower be!" And, to be honest, if people didn't need to borrow money, there wouldn't be money-lenders to get them into trouble. And, I suppose that if you are a fool enough to borrow money, well, you can't complain if you get into trouble. The old man was full of these sayings. Us older ones took notice of him, but the young fellow . . .'

And then with the air of someone who had said too much, he left me, leading the docile horse away with him.

I followed slowly, so slowly that by the time I arrived back at the stables, Pat had disappeared, and the stable lad, was busy brushing what I now thought of, with a shade of pride, as 'my horse', while singing a Christmas carol melodiously in the animal's ear. I walked across to the boy and boldly asked to 'have a go' at grooming the animal. The horse, I thought, seemed to be enjoying the rhythmic stroking of the brush and it might be a good way of making friends. I knew Dickens well enough to guess that, sooner or later, I would be persuaded to master my fears and remount the beast. I explained the matter to the boy, eliciting his help in building friendly relationships between me and the horse while I brushed the animal, and he replied, to my surprise, in a strong Irish accent.

'To be sure, you'd be very welcome.'

I was taken aback and before I could think, I blurted out, '*Aroo* from Cork?'

He laughed. 'I am, *aroo*?'

I couldn't resist it. 'How are the *praaties*?' I enquired with a broad smile.

'Who taught you that rubbish?' He was now the one to be taken aback.

'Mr Dickens, of course,' I said, and then he laughed also.

'He's great *craic*, that man, so he is!' He sounded affectionate and at ease. Fond of his employer and enjoying his job, I thought, and so I ventured to ask another question.

'What's your name, then, lad and how do you like working over here in England?'

'It's Ronan, sir, and I like it fine. Sure, isn't the place full of Cork men.' His answer had come quickly – with a broad smile initially, but then his face darkened.

I seized the opportunity. 'Someone was telling me that the man who was killed is also from Cork. You must have known him.'

'Not a bit of it.' The words came quickly and sounded defensive. 'Cork's a big place – about eighty thousand people in Cork city. Wouldn't know more than a few hundred of them. And we didn't live in the city. Had a farm outside the city, not far from the sea. Reared horses.'

It was plausible. Nevertheless, I could have sworn that he was uneasy about my question. And why did he not question me about how I knew that the dead man was from the city of Cork?

'Moneylender, so they tell me,' I said in a nonchalant fashion. 'Not too popular, these fellows, not on this side of the Channel anyway, and I don't suppose it's too different across the water in your own city.'

'You may be right,' Ronan said and there was a rigidity about the expression on his face and the hands that held the rope slid up and down restlessly. I began to feel a certain curiosity about him.

'What brought you over here to Kent?' I asked. When he looked hesitant and slightly embarrassed, I added, 'So who is looking after the horses now, with you over here working for Mr Dickens?'

He shrugged. 'What brings anyone across the water? A job, of course. And Pat here is my eldest brother. Nice place, here. Plenty more brothers at home. We go in for big families over in Ireland. In England, they say that the eldest son inherits the family farm, but in Ireland it's the youngest one. If you have ten or more in the family, the eldest would be getting tired of waiting while the youngest grows up.'

So, Pat and this younger boy were brothers; that was interesting and explained Pat's dislike of O'Connor if perhaps his brother had got into money troubles back in Cork. But there was an air of uneasiness about this young man, and his eyes were defensive, so I decided to leave the probing. None of my business, would be his perfectly justified feeling.

Nevertheless, I was resolved to make it my business. Most of the people here at Dickens' Christmas celebration were friends, or, at least, acquaintances of mine. If this murder was nothing to do with them, why then I was determined that it should not be laid at their door. The most helpful thing that I could do, at this stage, was to find out a multiplicity of motives and opportunities and, if possible, so confuse the police to the extent that, after a respectable interval, the matter would be quietly allowed to drop and the death of a stranger out there on that bleak marshland beside that heartrending grave of all those dead children, could be allowed to melt into the legend of the Cooling graveyard.

The connection of the two brothers from the turbulent city of Cork would be just a minor contribution to the mystery of the Christmas Marshland Murder.

'Dick,' I said as soon as I found him in the dining room where he was organizing the carol singers for Christmas Eve, 'Dick, could I have a quick word with you?'

'Certainly, my dear fellow, but first, give me your opinion. Which carol is the most suitable for the first carol singers' song, on our Christmas Eve expedition. "Silent Night" or "In the Bleak Midwinter"?'

'"Silent Night",' I said vigorously and without a moment's hesitation – always my way when my opinion was asked by Dickens on a topic which was very much a matter of individual taste. Any indecisiveness would, I knew from experience, bring in a period of cross-examination and endless debate. I glanced up at the sky and said, 'More snow in that sky. With some luck it will be falling when you go door-knocking. Should double the contributions. Snow at Christmas makes people feel good. Yes, "Silent Night" definitely.'

'"Silent Night", it is,' said Dickens to Arthur Sullivan in an equally decisive manner. He was, I reckoned, getting slightly tired of all the questions which came his way, as the organizer of this perfect Christmas celebration.

'Now, what can I do for you, my dear fellow?' he asked so affectionately that I took pity on him and seizing his arm in mine, I drew him away from the crowd of willing helpers who were all seeking his approbation and opinion on the multitudinous plans for the wonderful Gad's Hill Christmas Eve celebrations.

'Just a quick word,' I said as I escorted him into the library. It was a peaceful refuge – not a person there and a welcoming fire burning in the hearth.

I poured each of us a generous glass of sherry and handed one to my host.

'You look as if you could do with that, Dick,' I said affectionately. 'Now, down the hatch.'

'Happy Christmas, Wilkie,' he said mechanically and obediently swallowed the sherry.

In a few words, and as quickly as possible, I explained my plan to keep the police happy and to spread their enquiries into as many different avenues as I could uncover. I was a little apprehensive as Dickens was a man who liked to dictate rather than to acquiesce, but luckily he was so tired of having his opinion sought by all and sundry during the last few hours that he nodded obediently and even pronounced the words 'good idea' with a certain measure of enthusiasm. I thanked him and wished him a good evening with his carol singers.

'By the way, that young Irishman, Ronan, Pat's brother, has a good singing voice – heard him singing to that bad-tempered horse of yours,' I said; being well-known to be tone-deaf I thought that he might question my judgement but to my surprise he just looked pleased.

'Is that a fact,' he said enthusiastically. 'Well, we must certainly coax him into joining us tonight. Nice young fellow.'

'What made him come over to England to look for a job?' I asked, making sure that I introduced a casual note into my voice. Dickens was very loyal to those who worked for him and always very protective of his staff.

He shrugged his shoulders. 'Shortage of jobs over there. It's a distressful country – our fault perhaps. But at least we make up by providing jobs for all their young people.'

'Came in quite a hurry, though, didn't he?'

'You're not aiming to suspect him of anything, are you?' Dickens sounded irritated. 'Leave my staff out of it, Wilkie. They can't stand up for themselves. Anyway, he wasn't there on the marsh.'

Ah, but his brother Pat was, I thought, but I didn't voice my words.

He was silent for a few minutes, staring ahead of him with eyes which did not seem to see me, but which dwelt upon some strange picture in his mind's eye. I could have sworn that his mind was working so hard that he forgot my presence and was quite surprised when he addressed me in an absent-minded fashion.

'Come to think of it, Wilkie, didn't you notice that strange-looking man,' he said. 'I saw him so clearly – a fearful man – you must have seen him,' he went on in an undertone, not looking at me at all, but still gazing ahead with eyes that did not seem to be seeing any object but were engaged on some inner picture. 'Yes,' he said slowly. 'If you had seen him, you could not have forgotten him. A fearful man, all in coarse grey, with a great iron on his leg. A man with no hat, and with broken shoes and with an old rag tied round his head. A man who had been soaked in water and smothered in mud, and lamed by stones, and cut by flints and stung by nettles and torn by briars; who limped and shivered and glared and growled; and whose teeth chattered in his head . . .'

He continued this description in rhapsodic fashion and with a faraway look in his eye. It was such a terribly real picture of an evil-looking man – of a man who could easily have committed that brutal murder – that I stared at him open-mouthed.

'But, but, Dick,' I stammered. 'Why haven't you told the police about this man. It can't have been one of the convicts – he would not have been alone. They were all handcuffed to each other, shackled to each other. I saw them. And the guards, the guards with their whips and their bullhorns, they would never have allowed one man to wander off by himself. Where was it that you saw him?'

Dickens said nothing for a minute. He had heard my question; I was certain of that. But he still stared straight ahead, like one who is calling to mind a vivid image that had been imprinted upon his memory. I saw him nod. Not to me, but to himself.

'It *was* one of the convicts,' he said after that interval of silence and still with that strange, rhapsodic expression upon his face. 'He must have been an escaped convict,' he continued. 'He would have had shackles on his legs and these cuffs on his arms, but the metal had been broken, not cut, smashed by a stone, I would imagine. There was blood, too. That would make sense, wouldn't it? He wounded himself to free his limbs from the shackles. Blood on his leg and blood dried and hardened on his arm. That would be right. It would have been one of those huge heavy stones, of course. He would have hammered the shackles with it. The man was so desperate that he was willing to risk anything, was willing to smash his own limbs. He had to get free. At any cost to him.'

I gazed at him with excitement. Words poured from him. Only a gifted writer, I thought, could have given such a vivid description. *A fearful man, all in coarse grey, with a great iron on his leg. A man with no hat, and with broken shoes and with an old rag tied round his head. A man who had been soaked in water and smothered in mud, and lamed by stones, and cut by flints and stung by nettles and torn by briars; who limped and shivered and glared and growled; and whose teeth chattered in his head . . .* The words had seared themselves upon my memory. But I said nothing for a few moments as I saw that his eyes had darkened and that he was still scanning the picture in his mind's eye for more descriptions. But he had finished sharing them with me and he walked across the floor and stood by the window looking out at the thin veil of snow which covered the grass lawn and the hedges. Perhaps, he was recalling something else, was going to add another facet to the picture of the man on the lonely marshland.

'And then he saw the man who had been responsible for convicting him, responsible for his jail sentence, responsible for a living hell!' I suggested, but Dickens made no response. His eyes were still abstracted, and he seemed unconscious of my presence.

However, the picture he had drawn with his words had become quite real in my mind and after a few minutes I could wait no longer.

'Dick, the police must be told about this,' I said the words excitedly and it seemed as though the sound of my voice pulled Dickens from some sort of trance. He looked at me and for a moment, oddly, it almost appeared to me as though he were angry.

I looked back at him in puzzlement. Surely Dickens wanted the man caught and convicted? And then I understood. Of course, he wanted to see the police himself, give the description himself.

'You'll have to speak to the sergeant, yourself, Dick,' I said humbly. 'I'm afraid that I just didn't notice that strange convict, alone and unshackled from his companion. I'm sure that what you saw, must be, would be, a most valuable piece of information. The only problem will be,' I went on, now determined to warn him about the possible obstacles, 'I do fear,' I said, 'that the prison guards will not be pleased, may even flatly deny that such a thing was possible. And I must say that I, myself, saw no sign of a man such as you describe and especially not one convict on his own. It might bring a reprimand, or perhaps one of the guards might lose his job.'

By now Dickens was himself again. His colour had returned, and his eyes were no longer haunted. He looked at me affectionately.

'You're quite right, Collins. Yes, I think I will keep that picture of a convict locked in my head for the moment. You and I can discretely question some of our friends and see whether anyone else saw the man that I have just described. Perhaps, after all, he might just be a figment of my imagination.' For a moment it almost appeared as though he were amused, but I dismissed that from my mind as he took his notebook from his pocket and scribbled in it, his face, I noticed, was now very serious and wearing its most intent expression.

'And now my friend,' he said, 'just between us, I don't think that I feel like informing the police about any strange reaction that some of my guests showed to the late and not very lamented moneylender. *Moneylender*,' he repeated with an emphatic nod of his head. 'Yes, indeed, my friend, I picked up the trouble that he was causing and never regretted more heartily to have invited any guest to my house. I've had a guest who bored everyone, guests who dominated the conversation, guests who annoyed people, guests who would talk politics and expected everyone to be instantly converted to their doctrine, but I must say, Collins, that I have never before this Christmas had a guest who frightened my guests . . .' Dickens paused a few seconds and then added in a low voice, 'And who got himself murdered . . .'

I smiled, a little ruefully. 'You notice everything, Dick,' I said. My mind went to Georgina, but not even to Dickens, himself, would I betray her confidence. 'How are you going to manage?' I asked humbly.

'I'll use Charley, God bless the boy,' he said without a moment's hesitation. 'A lovely, affectionate fellow, my dear Charley, but with the worst memory that I have ever come across in my life.' Dickens paused for a moment, his face abstracted almost as though he were calling up the image of his eldest son.

'Nevertheless,' he said cheerfully, 'the great thing about Charley is that if you tell him he said something, or did something, he never replies with a denial, never argues. His response, dear boy, is always, "Oh, did I?" And so, I will quote Charley to the police. Charley, I will tell them, confided in his dear father, just before he rushed off to the household of that lady friend of his. This is what I will tell the police: Charley had noticed that several of my guests were inclined to shun the late lamented Timothy O'Connor. Like the good son that he is, Charley, before departing to spend Christmas with the girl whom he planned to marry, confided in his father about the behaviour of this strange Irishman and had even told him that he had heard somewhere or from someone that the man was an unscrupulous moneylender. However, the dear boy, without any prompting, will confide in the police that he just can't remember who said that.'

I was slightly confused by this. Charley, I seemed to remember, had spent minutes, rather than hours, with his father's guests and had escaped as soon as he possibly could. 'Did he know then about Timothy O'Connor?' I asked. 'Did he know him? Had he met him?'

Dickens watched me impatiently. 'No, of course, he didn't know him,' he said in a tone that completely ruled out any possibility that a son of his might have anything to do with moneylenders. 'I'm explaining to you, Collins – and I do wish you will listen. I shall tell the police that Charley told me that story and I shall tell them in the sure and certain knowledge that when my dear old Charley returns, I know exactly what he will say when the police question him. He will immediately look vague, will say, "Did I?" and then after a few minutes, he will add, very apologetically – Charley is always polite – "I'm afraid that I can't remember. What with Christmas and everything." Charley always has a good reason for forgetting things. But if the police tell him that he said these things to his father or to anyone else, he will immediately agree. Will be immensely relieved and assure them that his father has a great memory. He's a good boy. Has never been a troublemaker. Just slides through life. And, of course, the beauty of Charley is that if the police inspector asks him which one of the guests looked uncomfortable in the presence of Timothy O'Connor, Charley will instantly reply, as he always does, "I can't remember. I have a terrible memory".' Dickens laughed heartily and indulgently. He was fond of Charley; I knew that.

I let it go. Charley, I supposed, might be as docile as his father supposed. However, the 'boy' was no longer a boy, but a young man of over twenty years and about to set up business for himself. Myself, I would be quite uneasy about relying on a twenty-year-old who was absent-minded, in love, and having his mind filled with important changes in his life. It would, I thought, have been easier if Dickens had dropped a hint to Charley before he left the house.

Still, I told myself, I was probably worrying unduly. After

all, if Charley was uncertain about his own memory ability, he was unlikely to contradict his father to the police, no matter how far-fetched the story appeared to him. And, of course, it was true. There had been an uneasy feeling among all the guests. That was all that I had experienced myself and would be happy to report this rather useless impression to the police. Above all, I was determined not to involve Georgina.

# ELEVEN

B y the time that the police arrived to question the guests – the choir, the money collectors, the bell ringers, in other words most of the guests, except for the nephews of the dead man – were already dressed in the green cloaks and red scarves which Dickens produced from well-labelled shelves, within a neat cupboard in the hallway where Christmas decorations and Christmas costumes were kept from year to year. The police inspector and his two assistants seemed to be having a hard job to conceal their amusement at their festive appearance.

Hugely thankful to be excused from the embarrassing business of disturbing householders from their whiskey and mince pies, from their last-minute cooking, decorating Christmas trees, and present-wrapping, by demanding that they listen to a Christmas carol and pay for the unwanted choral visit, I had volunteered to stay at home in order to look after the police when they arrived and was so pleased to have escaped the carol singing that I bustled around with a great show of efficiency. I immediately allocated the morning room to them as a place where they could take statements from those of the guests who had visited Cooling graveyard. It was adequate but not over-warm, I noted with approval. There was, I felt, no point in making the police too comfortable. The correct procedure would be to treat them with deference and efficiency. I set out three chairs behind the table there and a couple of chairs opposite and added a substantial log to the fire, before re-joining the crowd in the hallway.

While Dickens and Arthur Sullivan debated over the choice of carols, I managed to scribble a quick list of those singers – only four of them, I was glad to see, who had also visited Cooling marsh and told them to have their stories ready for when called upon by the police. 'And keep it short,' I warned them. 'Nothing, unless it is relevant to the murder. And if you saw nothing relevant, heard nothing relevant, then for heavens' sake say it quickly and firmly and get this wretched carol singing over and the police out of the house as soon as we can.'

'Lucky Dickens has you to manage for him,' said Daniel Maclise who was hanging around the hallway. There was, I thought, a slightly sarcastic note in his voice to which I objected as I thought that out of all Dickens' numerous friends, I was the one doing the most to help him.

And then I remembered what Dickens had told me about that well-known artist, Daniel Maclise. Of course! He was born and brought up in the city of Cork and only came to London when he was in his twenties. Nothing in accent or demeanour now indicated that he was anything but a Londoner, but Dickens, in my experience of him, was always accurate.

'"*Aroo* from Cork?"' I said, and without waiting for an answer went on with the rhyming doggerel. '"How are the *praaties*?"'

He glared at me, and I smiled back, innocently.

'You're supposed to say, "big and *shmall*",' I pointed out with as good an imitation of a Cork accent as exemplified by Charles Dickens himself.

He didn't answer but walked off, stiff with outrage. I didn't pursue him. I was busy thinking. Why was he so annoyed? After all, what was wrong about being from Cork? A wonderful city, according to the famous author, Charles Dickens. Perhaps he thought the quote of the rhyming doggerel was in some way an offence to his native city. I couldn't see why. After all there were plenty of doggerels written about London so why take offence. Was there some reason why he did not want to be connected to Cork at this particular time, on a day when a man from Cork had just been murdered? That, I thought, was the more likely of my surmises.

It was, I thought, decidedly odd how Kent, the most English of counties, seemed, this Christmas, to have a lot of Cork men spending Christmas in the hospitable house of Charles Dickens and, of course, at the scene of a murder. Daniel Maclise had certainly been there. He had been one of two people whom I had noticed in the churchyard when Dickens and I were hurrying the two children back to shelter from the snow that had begun to fall. Daniel Maclise, I seemed to remember, had been alone, standing, not within the church, but outside it, appearing to be examining the outer wall of the porch, not far from that pathetic little grave, adorned by the statues laid there to commemorate the dead children. He had definitely been one of two people in the churchyard and the other, one of the twin nephews of the murdered man, had just been emerging from the shelter of a wall on the other side of the church. Had gone there for privacy to urinate, I guessed. I dismissed him from my mind and went back to thinking about Maclise who had been very near to the stone statues.

Still, would Daniel Maclise, a popular and best-selling artist, a man five or six years older than Dickens, have anything to do with a moneylender? I doubted it. Virtually impossible, I would have thought. Even Queen Victoria had bought one of his pictures to present as a birthday present to her beloved husband, Albert.

Unless, unless, there was something in his past, of course! After all, both men were from the city of Cork. Someone had told me once that Maclise, when not much more than a boy, had experienced great difficulty in getting the money together to come across the sea to London to enable himself to get the training that his genius craved. You only had to look at the determination in his eyes to know that he would be a success.

And, of course, I thought, now Daniel Maclise was at the top of his tree – so he had much to lose if any ugly rumour about him came to the notice of his wealthy patrons. It certainly would be worth police time to keep him in mind, though I myself doubted that a painter would be such a man of action as to smash to a pulp the body of an enemy.

But my aim was to accumulate as many people as possible who, because of a connection with the dead man (whether through place of origin or a history of money borrowing) might have some possible reason to kill him. Already there were his nephews – it would not take the police long to get their life story from them, I reckoned, but they would be in no real danger. It would, I decided, be hard to accuse all three young men and very easy for them to give alibis. They tended to keep themselves together in a tight little group, at a distance from the other guests and Dickens, the most convivial of hosts, had so far failed to integrate them into the jolly, carefree atmosphere of his Christmas celebrations.

I began to experience a thrill of interest when I counted all the guests and servants under Dickens' roof and realized how a large proportion might, in one way or another, at one time, have had some dealings with that unpleasant man. I could, I thought, create quite a confused picture for the police to grapple with.

I showed the police officers into the prepared interrogation room and gave them some background to the situation. I made sure that the police heard the whole story about the origin of the dead man from the city of Cork and the reason for his presence here in the famous writer's country house. Cork, I told them helpfully, was a city in the south of Ireland.

There was a smile on my face as I introduced Daniel Maclise himself to the police inspector. As I left the room, I heard him give his birthplace as Cork; a city in southern Ireland, he explained to them, and I could feel my smile grow as I heard the note of interest in the policeman's voice. The more that the word 'Cork' could be used, the more likely it was that the police would shelve the matter after a while.

With a slight smile on my face, I left Daniel Maclise to his interrogation and went to collect Georgina, Jas, his nephew George and William Willis.

The carol singers, once they had made their rapid depositions to the police, went off in an excited mood, all of them very cheered by the announcement that the landlord of the nearby public house had sent a boy to Gad's Hill with the promise that a warm welcome and a choice of drinks awaited them as a reward for a few well-sung Christmas carols at the Falstaff Inn.

'Here is the list of the rest of people who went on the walk to Cooling graveyard, but don't worry about it as I will be your runner and fetch anyone you want to question,' I assured the police, checking that Dickens' parlour maid had set out a tasty array of sweet mince pies, Christmas cake and a pot of tea to sustain. 'Anyone like a whiskey to keep the cold out?' I asked hospitably, waving the bottle with one hand, and lining up three glasses with the other. I saw them relax.

'Well, strictly speaking, sir, we shouldn't have alcoholic drinks,' said the inspector.

'Certainly not!' My voice, I could hear, sounded suitably horrified. 'Just a nice hot cup of strong tea,' I added, slipping a generous amount of whiskey into the three glasses. 'The tea might be too hot, and you can cool it with this stuff,' I explained, and the inspector merrily winked at me.

I would have loved to stay in the room, but it wasn't fair on the guests to have another guest listening in to their evidence. Hopefully, when I brought in fresh refreshments, I might be updated. I would also, I thought, facilitate them by making out a list of the visitors to the marshland.

As soon as the choir had left I came back to the police and they were extremely pleased to have my neat list.

'You're a very organized gentleman,' said one and I told him happily that he was the first one to pay me a compliment like that during my entire lifetime. There was a certain amount of laughter when I related what friends and relatives had said of me and one of the sergeants said that he would have a word with his superiors about offering me a job.

'But, of course, you are a famous author, aren't you and might be too busy for policework,' he added and I basked in his words, though suspecting that he might be mixing me up with Dickens. Still, I was pleased to have been found so efficient, so I bustled off to find Bertrand Chapman and to warn him that he would be next, reserving his nephew, kept sitting patiently in the corridor, for the number two victim. He was a bit of a wild boy, Jonathan Chapman; I had heard that from a friend of my younger brother. Keen on gambling, apparently, and I would not be altogether surprised to find that he could have been in the snares of a moneylender.

A while later, I went to go and seek out Bertrand Chapman, though if he were dozing by the fire then I would not wake him up, I resolved. Dickens should not have allowed him to walk all the way to Cooling Marshes even if it had been mostly downhill. He had looked very tired when he climbed onto the coach for the homeward journey.

Bertrand, however, was wide awake. Not reading, but sitting quite upright, poker in hand, deep in thought. He welcomed me with a smile.

'Just the man I wanted to have a chat with,' he said. 'I've just given my statement to that nice police inspector chap. All very quick and efficient. Now I find it's impossible to stop thinking about that affair this afternoon, is it not? He was, after all, a visitor in this house, his nephews were here . . .'

'And quite a few people seemed to have recognized him, don't you think?' I said eagerly.

He turned an interrogatory face to me, and I hastened to explain. 'You see, Bertrand, this fellow, this uncle of these young men, came from Cork city in the south of Ireland. He acquired quite a sum of money, by cheating his nephews.' And then I began to explain the whole story to him though I had a feeling that it was not new to him.

'Had you heard about this man?' I asked and he nodded.

'Yes, one of the nephews very kindly climbed up a ladder to fetch a book from the library for me and we got talking. Very nice young fellow. I was sorry for him and his brothers. Foolish of his father to make that will. He should have known what that man was like. But there you are, he probably didn't believe that anything would ever happen to him while his children were young. One doesn't, you know. Doctors give opinions, but human optimism always prevails. One probably has to be near to the end before one believes that doctors are telling the truth,' he said with a wry smile and I felt very sorry for him.

'Of course, if they tell the police about this, do you think it will give a motive for the murder, in their eyes, anyway?' I asked, feeling that it would distract him from his troubles to speculate about who killed the unpleasant Timothy O'Connor.

Bertrand pursed his lips. 'I doubt it,' he said. 'It is a little too far-fetched. But let's put our mind to it. Tell me all that you know about the late and not particularly regretted victim.'

I told him all that I knew about the man, and he listened very carefully, nodding his head from time to time. I even trusted him enough to tell him about Georgina's troubles, but when I swore him to secrecy he smiled and shook his head at me.

'Poor Georgina,' he said in an amused fashion. 'She does like to share her troubles. I suppose you got the full story over dinner, did you?'

'You don't mean that she told you, also!' I was taken aback, but then I, too, smiled. Georgina probably was one of those people who could never resist the opportunity to share her troubles.

'Surely not Georgina,' he said, as he read my mind and watched me dip the pen into the ink to start a new list of suspects.

'Well, they are going to interview everyone who was there and there were not too many women so I might as well put her down. No, I don't think that she did it, but . . .'

'Not Georgina!' he repeated firmly. 'I could not imagine her capable of such a deed. Georgina would always expect someone else to do the deed for her.'

'A bit dangerous to go around telling everyone her troubles if she were the one that rolled the stone,' I said, 'but remember it was probably a spur of the moment deed. No one could have planned that murder. No one could have imagined that a man would fall asleep just downhill from that pathetic little grave. And, of course, Georgina is just the type of person to do things on the spur of the moment.'

He looked surprised. 'Surely it would have been too heavy for a girl,' he said.

I shook my head. 'Not according to Dickens' son, Walter. He had some scientific reason that he put forward that proved that given a rounded object, and given that steep slope, in the graveyard as well as on the hillside, well, a child could have done the deed.'

Bertrand thought about that for a moment or two, his forehead creased into lines of worry.

'Perhaps he was trying to distract you, trying to lay emphasis on the possibility that anyone there on that marsh could have done the deed, man or woman.'

'Distract me,' I said feeling slightly puzzled.

'I hope to goodness that none of these young men got

themselves into trouble with that scoundrel,' said Bertrand. He hadn't directly answered my question, but he had certainly put another idea forward.

I thought about it for a moment and then shook my head decisively. 'No, Walter told me that his father always came to the rescue if they needed money to fulfil a debt or something like that. He did say that he would read them a lecture, which does sound like Dickens, but that when it came to it, he would always get them out of trouble.'

Bertrand raised his eyebrows, and I could sense doubt oozing from him, but he said nothing, other than a perfunctory, 'Good, good.' I made a few notes, adding 'young men' as a blanket group and then moved the conversation on. I did want plenty of possible candidates for the police to think about, but I didn't want to get into trouble Walter, who had been so open and so friendly with me. I would not, I thought, list him separately.

'What about Daniel Maclise?' I queried. 'Same city. Might be some scandal, some boyish crime, or even some illicit love affair that he would not want revealed seeing that wealthy men now trust him to paint pictures of their wives and daughters. Quite a position of trust, if you think about it. Sitting there, hour after hour, day after day. Something might have happened in his youth in Cork when he was a young man. He might have seduced a girl or a young woman. Maclise, I'm sure that someone told me, had done quite a few portraits in his native city before he came across to London.'

'Good,' said Bertrand with a nod. 'Yes, give him a place on your list. The police will question him, but they won't trouble him too much. The man is far too famous. And with the number of portraits he sells, I doubt that he ever needs the service of a moneylender, but then, as you say, fame brings problems. No one would ever bother gossiping about me, but they would about Maclise and Dickens and you, yourself, of course, now that you have had such success with your novels,' he finished politely.

That gave me an idea and so I began to make my list. I began by having two columns, one for famous and one for not famous, but as faces came into my head I realized that most of Dickens' visitors, except for his last-minute invitees from Ireland, were quite famous in London.

'Should I put women down?' I asked.

'Yes, why not, the more the merrier,' said Bertrand with a broad smile and, although he laughed at the suggestion, for good measure I added as many women as I could remember. In his kind, slightly old-fashioned way, I had the strong feeling that Bertrand thought it was ridiculous to have women on the list, but that, I thought, would be up to the police.

'Of course, Wilkie,' he said after a minute, 'they say that poison is a woman's weapon. I'll tell you something interesting that I read recently, and it was that between 1843 and 1852 – just nine years, Wilkie – seventeen women, yes seventeen, have been executed for poisoning! What do you think of that? Seventeen women in less than ten years! Gives you a bit of a shock, doesn't it? But come to think of it, it's jolly easy to murder someone by poisoning, especially if you are the one who does the cooking, or you are the mistress of the house and would not excite any attention if you check on the plates, re-arrange the food, offer a particular dainty to the person that you want to murder. And women have an annoying habit of forcing you to eat something or other which they tell you will do you good.'

'Georgina does that,' I said, suddenly remembering the rather pleasant feeling I had experienced when she had once popped some sweetmeat into my mouth after dessert had been served. But I wasn't murdered, and no one was poisoned either.

'Exactly,' said Bertrand with a smile. 'And so, I think that we can rule out the women. If any one of the women had wanted to murder that unpleasant man, why they would have poisoned him. You know what it's like, poisoning is definitely a woman's crime.'

He seemed pleased with his conclusion and so I left it. I was not quite convinced, though. It struck me that it would not be so easy for a woman to use poison in someone else's house. In addition, the use of the stone statue which lay on a grave at the top of the hill, just above where an evil and much hated man had fallen into a drunken slumber, had been an opportunist crime and could have been the work of either

a man or a woman. And, I did feel that, given the frozen
ground and the very steep slope of compacted sand and earth
that had been firmed down by the feet of the convicts, that
anyone, man, woman, or young boy could have sent the stone
effigy on its deadly path. Once that stone had begun to roll
then it would gather speed and become a deadly instrument
of death.

'What was it like in the church?' I asked him, adding,
'before we, Dickens and myself, arrived back, I mean,'

'Not very jolly,' he said with a smile. 'I suppose most people
were wishing that they had not come, and were wondering,
as I know that I was, why we had not all gone home once the
grave had been admired and the lunch consumed. I was feeling
exasperated with Dickens, thinking that it was typical of him
to have gone off for a long walk when any sensible person
would have looked at the sky and seen the prospect of snow.
But, of course, I should have known better than to come. The
last time that I stayed with Dickens, quite a number of years
ago, he walked us all from Folkestone to Dover, and then back
again and just to add a touch of spice to the expedition, the
tide was coming in rapidly when we reached the Warren
outside Folkestone harbour, but he insisted on starting a hunt
for pre-historic fossils among the rocks and on the slope of a
lethal-looking cliff and offering a prize for the best collection!
And all the time while he gave one of his wonderfully lucid
descriptions of the fossils which we could find, I was feeling
the sea creeping up onto the toe of my boots, And, if I remember
rightly, it was while he was explaining the difference between
an *ammonite* and a *belemnite* that one of those freak waves
came rushing up the beach and everyone was soaked to
knee-level.'

I laughed. I couldn't help it. It was all so like Dickens. A
large proportion of our London friends would have similar
anecdotes to relate about their sojourns under Dickens' hospitable roof. Of course, the odd thing was that no one ever
refused an invitation. No matter what happened, no matter
how short, a stay with Dickens was bound to provide anecdotes
that would last for months.

'Mind you,' I said teasingly. 'Snow, or no snow, I would

have preferred to be walking across the marshland with
Dickens, listening to his conversation and to the sound of the
waves, where the sea meets the River Medway, rather than
sitting in the icily cold church and staring at an altar. Did
everyone just sit there, or were people popping in and out?'

'I suppose that they were.' Bertrand considered the matter.
'Call of nature, et cetera. Yes, there was a certain amount of
movement. The place was damn cold, you know, so although
some sat, most people moved around a bit, looked at the
statues and the paintings, and the stone tablets, or went in
and out. I went outside once, but it was bitterly cold and so
I came back in again quite quickly. And now, my dear fellow,'
he said, getting to his feet, 'would you think it very rude of
me if I deserted you and went off to bed. I have an uneasy
feeling that if our host returns soon, or even any time before
midnight, I may be persuaded into joining a game of Poor
Pussy or even, worse still, of Grandmother's Footsteps. I feel
my bed and a book is calling me and last night I had the
pleasant experience of finding an enormous copper bed
warmer had made my bed extremely pleasant. Dickens, dear
fellow, came up with me to make sure that it had not been
forgotten and when I went up for a clean handkerchief an
hour ago, I found one of the maid servants already slipping
it under the bedclothes.'

I wished him good night and was left with a warm feeling
of affection for Dickens. He had a multitude of annoying
practices, could be dictatorial, but he was a wonderful friend.
I wonder whether anyone else of our acquaintances, on top of
all those elaborate arrangements for Christmas jollifications,
would think of checking that his order to supply an enormous
copper bed warmer for a guest who did not look well was
fulfilled.

Dickens had, also, I presumed, given other special instructions to his staff as, after Bertrand had left the room, I heard
a servant in the hallway asking him whether he would like to
have some warm milk, or a cup of tea. I could tell that Bertrand
was touched by the offer, but he assured her that he was
thinking of pouring himself a small whiskey and beseeching
her not to let anyone know.

She was still laughing when she came in to attend to the fire.

'What a nice gentleman, he is,' she said to me. 'Not looking too well, though, is he? Pulled down by the hard winter. He'll feel better when the sun comes back again. Once Christmas is over, we'll all be looking forward to the spring, won't we, sir?'

'You're having a lot of work with all the visitors,' I said sympathetically, but she brushed my words away with a wave of her hand.

'It's a pleasure,' she said. 'I love to see people enjoying themselves. Working for Mr Dickens is a pleasure. We feel part of the family, if you'll excuse me saying that, sir.'

'I think Mr Dickens would be delighted to hear you say that,' I said, and I knew that I was speaking the truth.

'He's a very kind master. Came into the kitchen to ask that lad from the stables, the boy from Cork city in Ireland, would he join in the singing, asked it as a favour, too, not told him to do it like most masters would do. Very pleased the boy was to be asked. I could see that. His face lit up. Missing his family, I'd say. And, I wouldn't say this to anyone but you, sir, but I did see Mr Dickens slip him a sovereign.'

She was a nice woman, and like many of her sex and age, a great talker. I thought that I might probe her knowledge of the household, especially about this young lad from Cork.

'Quite a young age to leave your family and your country – looks not more than fifteen or sixteen at the most,' I said carelessly. I poured myself a whiskey and then held the bottle over a second glass and raised an eyebrow at her.

'Keep me company?' I asked in a casual fashion.

She hesitated a little, but Dickens' staff were used to being treated a bit like one of the family and she couldn't resist the sharp sweet aroma.

'You're very kind, sir,' she said and rapidly I filled the glass.

'Happy Christmas!' I lifted my glass and touched it to hers.

'Happy Christmas, sir and many happy returns,' she said.

I had once heard some woman ask Dickens how on earth he kept a full staff during the Christmas period. Her staff, she told him, always wanted to go home.

'This place is home to my staff,' had been his reply and,

oddly, I would not be surprised if his staff would give the same answer. I perched on the edge of the table, and she perched on the windowsill and there was enough of a relaxed atmosphere between us, as we sipped our whiskey, to allow me to pick up the conversation in an offhand way.

'Yes,' I said. 'I wouldn't put him at more than about fifteen, myself. I wonder what made him leave his family home.'

She drank some more of the whiskey with the air of someone who is a connoisseur. I refilled her glass.

'Mind you, I remember myself when I was fifteen . . . remember what I was like . . .' I said, disguising the vagueness of my pronouncement by swallowing back some more of the whiskey.

'Well, you know what it's like,' she said echoing my words while nodding her head. 'Boys will be boys. They get into trouble and, you know, the Irish are a wild lot, and there's many a one, so they say, who will slip out of trouble easily by getting the boat to England.'

'It wasn't anything very much, though, was it,' I said, adding a little more whiskey to my glass and then topping up hers, also.

She gave me a conspiratorial nod.

'It would have blown over if that fellow hadn't made trouble, so I heard,' she said.

'Pity Mr Dickens asked him here for Christmas.' It was a long shot, but I thought that I would try it. 'Stirring things up again, that's what he was after.'

'Made nothing but trouble from the time that he arrived!' she agreed. Then she added indulgently, 'Of course, Mr Dickens wouldn't believe any harm of a man that he had invited into his own house, but I could have told him how that fellow was poking around, poking here and there. Recognized Pat's young brother, so someone told me, when he came into the kitchen for a cup of tea after raking the dead leaves from the lawn. "You here! Does Mr Dickens know all about you?" That's what he said, sir, and the poor young fellow turning as white as my apron, so I was told. Couldn't say a word. And Pat looking from one to the other. Not a one to speak before he thinks, that's Pat. I tell him sometimes that he is no Irishman. Most of the Irish speak out almost before they draw breath, but he's not like that. He thinks before he speaks – that's Pat for you. And you can bet that if he didn't speak out, well there was a reason for it. No smoke without fire. My mother used to say that, sir. She was a great one for sayings was my mother. Always had one on the tip of her tongue. She was Welsh, so she was.'

My new friend had something of the Welsh in her, also, I thought. English servants were not as garrulous as that in the usual way of thing. However, I was anxious to encourage her so I nodded and said, 'Must have given Pat a bit of shock, too, did it?'

'That it would have, sir. I got that feeling. Lucky for the young fellow that he had his brother with a job in England if there had been a bit of trouble back in Ireland. Easy to get the boat to England but not always easy to get a job. They say that there are lots of Irish who are homeless on the streets of London.'

'And that's not something that I would wish on my worst enemy,' I said.

'Nor I.' She shivered a little. 'Not on a night like this, sir,' she said. 'But Mr Dickens is generous like that. If a man is good with horses, like Pat is, and a younger brother turns up, well, Mr Dickens would give him a try. That's the sort of man that he is. Not all employers are like that.'

And with a nod, she picked up her tray and left me to my thoughts. A sharp-eyed girl, I thought, and I was fairly sure that she suspected that Pat's younger brother might have been in trouble in his native city and had taken the boat for England instantly. I experienced a warm feeling of appreciation for my friend. Yes, indeed, not all employers would take a new servant on without a reference. But, of course, if it were proved to Dickens that the boy had committed some crime, why that would have been a different matter. Dickens was, I knew, very straitlaced when it came to matters of breaking the law. And, of course, he had his own young teenage sons: Charley, Walter, Frank and Sydney. He could not risk introducing anyone who had committed a crime into his household.

If the moneylender, Timmy, had told him that Pat's younger brother was wanted by the police, he would not, I was sure, keep him in his household. And, if there was a danger of his brother being left homeless, Pat, who had been keeping warm by walking around the land by the graveyard while Dickens and his guests explored the marshlands, well, perhaps he, on seeing that unpleasant man sunk into a drunken stupor, might well have seized the opportunity of safeguarding his young brother and getting rid of the threat.

# TWELVE

D ickens and the carol singers were noticeably cheerful when they arrived home. The police had disappeared, promising to leave us in peace over Christmas Day – so said the inspector. I had gone to the front door a few times after the police had left, wondering whether I should go to bed when I heard the melodious voices singing, 'God Rest Ye, Merry Gentlemen!' and then I saw the torches held by Pat and his young brother. The snow had begun to fall again, not heavily but just snowflakes drifting gently down and alighting upon the green cloaks and the red scarves. It made a lovely picture, but I was too worried to enjoy the spectacle. I noticed that at the sight of me, Dickens had ceased singing and with a word to Daniel Maclise, he came swiftly towards me.

'All well,' he said and there was a strong note of anxiety in his voice.

'All goes well,' I said. 'Nice quiet evening.' I was about to add a joking sentence about there being no murders to report but by the light of the lantern which he held I could see his face quite clearly and there was an expression of anxiety upon it. Not a moment for jokes, I decided. Dickens was a man who took the responsibility of host very seriously.

'Bertrand has gone to bed, but I thought I would wait up for you all,' I said, and he nodded. He still looked anxious, I thought, and I could understand that. After all, though he had been an unpleasant man, nevertheless, the murdered money-lender had been a guest in his household and an uncle to three of the present guests.

The three nephews, though, now that I could see them, did not seem to be mourning, but were singing with great gusto, as was Pat's young brother who had a wonderfully sweet tenor singing voice. He and Georgina were walking side by side, blending their voices into a most melodious sound.

'Was the Falstaff public house pleased with you?' I asked, sharing my question among the straggling procession.

'Said we should be on the stage in the West End of London,' boasted Georgina and I saw the young Irishman, Pat's brother, smile with pleasure. He did not stop singing and Georgina picked up the note from him and continued to sing in a most carefree manner. Although I was not particularly musical, I could tell that he and Georgina were creating a very pleasant sound. She was, I was glad to see, looking very well, full of the Christmas spirit. In fact, there was such an atmosphere of exhilaration ebbing from all the carol singers that I felt half sorry that I had not gone out with them, even if it were only to have held the collecting box.

'How is Bertrand?' asked Dickens in an undertone.

I was quite touched that, with all his cares and with all his responsibilities for his household, his children and his visitors, he still remembered the one visitor who was in poor health that might need some special care. Dickens could be exasperating, and it was possible to find a hundred faults in him, but he had a very kind heart and once a friend, you were of the utmost concern to him if you were unwell or in any sort of trouble.

'He's fine. Gone off to bed early with a bedwarmer to make everything cosy for him. One of your servants was offering him hot drinks as he went up the stairs,' I said reassuringly and was glad to see Dickens nod his head and smile at that news. I had the impression that he mentally ticked off one piece of responsibility before turning to another. He looked back, surveying his guests and for once there was a hint of doubt on his tired face.

'What do you think,' he said in an undertone. 'Should we play a few games before going to bed. What about Grandmother's Footsteps or Sardines?'

I shuddered inwardly at the thought and hastened to reassure him.

'I'm sure they are all tired out now. Everybody has the means to have a drink in their bedroom and if I were you, I'd let them go to bed while the memory of a very successful evening is fresh in their minds,' I said rapidly and was rewarded by a relieved smile on his tired face.

'You're right,' he said and raised his voice, turning back to face Arthur Sullivan. 'One last carol, and then a good night and a happy Christmas to everyone. Arthur, could you start us off.'

And Arthur Sullivan raised his melodious voice and began to sing, 'In the Bleak Midwinter' and all joined in with him. The carol brought all to the doorway before the last words were sung and by some miracle, they all dispersed, still singing softly as they climbed the stairs, quietly calling 'Happy Christmas' to each other before disappearing into their bedrooms.

'Happy Christmas, Dick,' I said, before I followed them up the stairs. But I was not surprised, ten minutes later, to hear a soft knock upon the door.

'Come in, Dick,' I said. He was, of course, bearing a tray with some slices of Christmas cake, a couple of glasses and a bottle of whiskey.

'I thought that you might like some of this whiskey, it's a new discovery of mine,' he said.

'I'd love to,' I said, without bothering to glance at the label. I was no connoisseur, but I could tell by Dickens' worried face that he needed to share his worries.

'Successful evening?' I queried accepting a brimful glass. And then when he did not reply, I added, 'How did that young fellow, Pat's younger brother, the boy from Ireland, how did he turn out?'

That unlocked the memories of the evening. 'Great singer and a great character!' he said enthusiastically. 'Life and soul of the party. Telling funny stories about taking the parish priest carol singing and feeding him with poteen which, I gather, is what we English call moonshine. Poteen, apparently means "little pot" but it's a whiskey made from potatoes left to ferment inside the pot until it is strong enough to blow the top of your head off, according to the young fellow, Pat's brother.' Dickens stopped and I knew by the expression upon his face that he was mulling over the conversation of the evening and teasing out a character profile for the latest member of his household.

'Very nice young fellow,' he broke his silence with a smile

upon his face and with a note of decisiveness in his voice.
'Ronan is his name. Much more talkative than Pat. Quite the
life and soul of the party. He made a great story about this
poteen. He was telling us how he himself and a cousin, while
still at school if you please, took some of his father's potatoes
and sealed them into a pot which they hid in the stables and
how they managed to make great poteen from them. Kept
them in the pot until they fermented, and then sold small
bottles of it to the neighbours, and even got the parish priest
to have a drink on a cold night when they were out carol
singing according to him. But then Pat gave him a dig in the
ribs to shut him up. Pat is a man to keep his own counsel.
Didn't like the story about the parish priest, and maybe thought
that Ronan was coming out of himself a bit too much for a
new boy. Quite a lad, this young Ronan,' said Dickens
reflectively.

'And a protective older brother,' I said thoughtfully. The
story about the illicit alcohol and the tricking of a parish
priest was perhaps not the most appropriate to be told on the
first week of work at a new job. Ronan, I thought, had a
reckless streak in him. It was little wonder that Pat was
protective about him. But how far would a man go to protect
a young brother? It depended, I thought, about what the secret
was. Why did Ronan leave Ireland so abruptly that he turned
up at his brother's workplace without a sending notice or
asking permission from his father or ensuring that a job would
await him. After all, the penny post was amazingly efficient.
There would not have been much delay if he had to wait for
his brother's reply. But, of course, I told myself, there are
certain situations when even a few hours' delay could be fatal.
Once again I wondered what was the true reason for that
abrupt decision.

'Let's talk about the murder,' I said impulsively. 'After all,
you and I walked the length and breadth of that desolate
marshland between the church and the village. The only people
we saw were the convicts and their guards and those of your
guests who walked across from Gad's Hill. Let's face it, Dick,
these convicts were extremely well guarded. They were
shackled together, and each had a warder within a few feet.

Did you, at any time of the morning or afternoon, see a single convict without a guard and a shackled companion? Of course, you didn't because there were none. I would be surprised if the police don't know how well guarded the convicts are, as well as we do ourselves. They were bound to have visited the marshland from time to time. After all the safety of the villagers and outlying houses like that of the blacksmith and his wife, all these people would have to be guaranteed safety or there would have been a fuss about allowing convicts to leave the ship, about using convicts on the shore. And the complaints would have come from the church and its vicar as well as from the people themselves.'

'You've made your point,' said Dickens with a note of slight impatience in his voice. 'Now tell me who murdered the moneylender whom I so stupidly invited into my own house and allowed to mix with my friends and my family.'

I said nothing for a moment. It was true that his impulsiveness had given rise to that unpleasant situation in which he had landed his family and his guests. I thought it over once more and could see no way out of this mess. There was no doubt but that, in the eyes of the police, his guests, and perhaps more important, his two teenage sons, Walter and Frank, could be under suspicion. There was a note of strain in Dickens' voice.

'Well,' I said. 'There are quite a few likely suspects. And there would have been an opportunity. Someone could have come out of the church for some fresh air or to relieve their bladder,' I said. 'They, man or woman, could have seen the moneylender lying in a drunken stupor, on top of that flat slab of rock and could have suddenly thought of using one of the statues as a weight to knock the brains from the man. Once the idea had come, its execution would have taken only a few minutes. I had remarked before, and you must have, too, Dick,' I said earnestly, 'on how well-made, how firm that path was. The convicts had made an excellent job of it by hammering the layers of sand into the marshland mud. In fact, that path was almost as if it had been made from concrete. That statue, of course, had been carved quite crudely from a piece of limestone but it had been rounded by the stormy wind and waves. It was the shape and size of a section of tree trunk, and it would have rolled down the steep path,' I finished, and then added, 'and it would have gained speed and momentum, as it went and there certainly was enough weight in it to knock the brains out of any man if it came down that steep slope and crashed into him.'

'And Pat, sitting there on the cart, or else walking around the marsh, not accompanied by anyone else, could be in a prime position,' said Dickens thoughtfully. 'He could have had a quick look around just to check that there was no one within sight of him, could have slipped across from the roadway, and onto that dark, flat wilderness beyond the churchyard. Yes,' said Dickens, now sounding quite emphatic, 'yes, I can see the scene.' He stayed very still, glass in hand, looking not at me, not at the fire, not at anything in the room, but at some far distant scene within his own imagination. After a few moments, he shook his head as though to clear a scene from it and returned his eyes to me. There was an appraising look in them and I looked back with interest.

'I can just see the scene, too. You do paint a picture,' I said, and he smiled and took a sip from his glass. 'The only difficulty is what would Pat's motive be?'

'That's easy,' he returned. 'Brotherly love.'

I pursed my lips. 'I'm very fond of my brother, but I don't think that I would commit a murder for him. I'd find the money to get him out of the moneylender's tendrils, perhaps, but I wouldn't murder anyone for him.'

'*Tendrils*!' he mocked. 'Come on, Collins, you can do better than that. I thought that you were setting up to be a writer.'

I ignored him. 'Never mind,' I said. 'You are probably right. Let's write down everything we can think about possible suspects and then weed out the most improbable.'

Dickens had a kind habit of always leaving a notebook and pencil in each guest bedroom. Many of his friends were writers and even for those who were not, there was always the possibility of a guest wanting to make a memorandum of a task to be done, or the name of a superb whiskey to be noted. I tore out a page and folded it to make three columns and inscribed a heading for each: Name, Motive, Opportunity.

And in the first line of each column I wrote: Pat. Brother/ blackmail? Alone in cart. 'I noticed that he went back there straight after the lunch, didn't you. I noticed him sitting there before we set off for our walk.'

I held the page up to him and Dickens thoughtfully poured himself another glassful and topped up mine. He said nothing. He was, I knew from experience, mentally testing my words and seeking to find a weak spot. I waited patiently. His brain, I knew, was a better brain than mine and over the years of our friendship I had grown to respect his conclusions about any matter to which he put his mind. And so, I sipped the whiskey and awaited his judgement.

'Well, at least we can give each other an alibi,' I said eventually, to break the silence, 'but unfortunately,' I added, 'that can't extend to your guests or to your employee, the stable lad. Nevertheless, Pat, I'm sure is an affectionate brother . . .' I allowed my sentence to tail out, not being quite sure about what point I wished to make.

'Reminds me of myself,' said Dickens. 'I was like Pat, always dragging my young brothers out of trouble. Cost me money sometimes when I could ill afford it.'

'But . . .' I paused after that word and then continued, looking at him very directly in the eyes, 'But, I don't suppose that you would have gone so far as to commit murder for them, would you?'

There was a silence in the room after these words of mine. Dickens did not laugh or even exclaim. He sat very still, staring ahead of him and then after a couple of minutes, he drank some wine from his glass.

'No,' he said. 'And, you know, Collins, I don't think that I would have been, for even one single minute, tempted to commit murder to get one of them out of trouble. I would certainly have considered that as being very much outside the bounds of brotherly love. And Pat, I understand, has five brothers. They have big families over there in Ireland. And you know what it is like in families. If I committed a murder for one of my brothers, they would all be wanting the same service and I'm sure that both Pat and I would draw the line at multiple murders of behalf of brothers.'

I laughed at that and was glad that he had said it. For a moment there had been an oddly uncomfortable feeling in the room and Dickens had worn an expression of resentment and anxiety. His birth family: father, mother, brothers and sisters cost him much in money and anxiety, even when he had a large family of his own.

Nevertheless, I thought, this matter of the murdered man, with connections to his household as well as to his guests, did need to be talked over. There was something that needed to be cleared away first and I tackled it instantly, swallowing some of the very strong whiskey before I began.

'This convict that you described to me, will you describe him to the police?' I asked mischievously.

For a moment he looked at me in a strange manner. It was not an angry, or even irritated manner. I could have sworn that there was a certain degree of pleasure in his expression.

'No, Collins, I won't,' he said gravely. 'To be honest, I don't think that description was relevant to the murder – more like something from a novel, perhaps? What do you think?'

I felt a certain relief. Unless we were quite sure of the guilt of an individual convict, I did not think it was fair to give such a very striking description of one man – a description so striking that it had to be taken from life. I could imagine the sound of whips striking on a bare back and the agony of suffering that an innocent man might have to endure. I looked at him in a slightly puzzled way. He sat back in his chair, his chin tilted, his face almost parallel with the ceiling and I could swear that, momentarily, a slight smile passed over his lips before disappearing behind an expression of solemn thoughtfulness.

'Mind you, Dick,' I said, 'the police will certainly interview the convicts and their keepers, but I'd like to think that it would not result in further suffering for the poor fellows and if the keepers all swear that the men were shackled and that they were never out of their keeper's sight, then it's going to be hard for the police to fasten anything on one of them, especially if someone of your stature and reputation is taking an interest in the case.'

That last sentence would, I hoped, have the effect of

spurring Dickens into becoming an active player in the search for the murderer of the moneylender. Certainly, he was struck by my words.

'Yes,' he said slowly. 'I can paint the scene for them: the dark flat wilderness beyond the churchyard, intersected with dykes and mounds and gates, with scattered cattle feeding on it, was the marshes; and that low leaden line beyond, was the river; and that distant savage lair from which the wind was rushing, was the sea . . .' Suddenly Dickens stopped, his eyes lost their strange appearance and he seemed to become conscious of my presence.

'Yes, indeed,' he said with an air of satisfaction, 'I think I can paint that scene and I think that it might play a part in my greatest book.'

I was lost in admiration. What a genius that man was! All that I, and anyone else whom I knew, could have said about that place was that it was a dreary marsh with a small church and churchyard perched upon its highest spot, but his description made it seem like something in the most thrilling of books. Perhaps, I thought with a sudden flash of insight, this terrible affair of the marshes, convicts, the prison ship and the murdered man, perhaps someday all of this will come together in a book and it will be read by millions for years to come.

'Dick,' I said impulsively, 'you with your wonderful brain, surely you have some idea who it was who committed that murder. It wasn't a convict. Both you and I know that is impossible, so it must have been one of our party, it must have been one of the group of people who, on this Christmas Eve morning, walked or rode upon a cart from Gad's Hill to this lonely spot.' I paused and looked at him. He had a tight smile upon his face and his eyes were the eyes of one who is looking upon a scene far from the cosy bedroom where we sat and drank his vintage whiskey. It took a few moments before he turned to look at me.

'Rode upon a cart,' he repeated in slightly mocking tones. 'So, which of those who rode upon a cart would you fancy for a murderer? My little Plorn, sweet little innocent that he is, or the Butler. I must confess that my money would be on the Butler. She has that streak of unscrupulous determination that must be of huge advantage if you want to commit a murder.'

'Don't be stupid,' I said angrily. 'I wasn't talking about children. You know that.'

I began to wish that I had never gone on this expedition to the Cooling Marshes and certainly that I had never brought my innocent little Carrie to such a scene. This murder had to be solved, I told myself. If it were not solved then the shadow of that mutilated corpse would, for years to come, hang over the memories of those who had been present on that day.

'Was Georgina capable of doing such a deed?' I said and recognized that there was a harsh note in my voice.

'Oh, I think so,' said Dickens coolly. 'I understand that she was in debt to the man, or so she told my wife, people like Georgina always tell the most intimate details about themselves to all and sundry – have you noticed that, Wilkie? And I'll tell you why,' he went on before I had a chance to answer him, 'that is because basically they think that they are the most important personage in their little world and since that man was making her unhappy by demanding that she repay the capital sum of money and the interest, of course, why then since he was making her unhappy, depriving her of her innocent pleasures like Parisian dresses and exquisite fur coats, not to mention all the other features in her extravagant lifestyle, well, of course, since she is of the utmost importance, it was essential that he was removed from her life and therefore, instantly the idea of the means to kill him came to her hand, so as to speak, why she acted without hesitation. I can just see her,' finished Dickens with a flourish as he poured another spoonful of whiskey into my glass and then into his own.

I made no comment. It was impossible to argue with Dickens. And, there was, I had to admit, a certain truth about the picture which he had painted of Georgina's attitude to life.

Nevertheless, we had to look at the possibility of any man or woman committing the deed who was present on the Cooling marshland. It was, I told myself, such a simple way to commit a murder. Even though the result was so appallingly gory, the process itself was a simple one which kept the murderer at a considerable distance from the bloody deed itself, just pushing a heavy stone down a hill, not at all like cutting a throat with a knife or a sword. It was, I thought, a murder which even a fastidious woman like Georgina could commit without a shudder. Set the stone rolling and then leave the rest in the hands of the deity which controls life and death. I voiced my thoughts aloud and Dickens nodded.

'It's quite possible that whoever committed that murder did not even stay to watch whether a sleeping or unconscious man was killed,' he remarked. 'Makes it more a woman's murder in a way. Women, in my experience,' said Dickens with the air of an expert, 'are far more likely to commit a crime where a certain element of chance enters into the process. Why, bless my soul, I've often seen my daughter Katy shut her eyes if she has been offered a choice between two presents. Or else it is all this "Eeny, meeny, miny, moe" business! The number of times, I've heard my two daughters chanting this, but never, even once, noticed it from my boys. They take after me. Grab what they want and grab it quickly in case they should lose it to one of their brothers and, though I should hope that not one of them will ever be tempted to murder an enemy, except in the cause of a just war; well, I should hope that in that eventuality, they would do the deed without any shilly-shally business. But, you see, Collins, a woman wants to get rid of that scoundrel, she sees him lying there, dead drunk, she hears him snore, she sees the stone pillar and says to herself, "Well, if that heavy stone rolled down that steep path it would smash into him, and it might just kill him. Wouldn't that be fortunate if that happened?"' Dickens paused, half-smiled to himself at the picture that his fertile mind was creating. He rubbed his hands for a minute before recommencing. 'And with a woman, my dear Wilkie,' he said in his usual positive tones of voice, 'with a woman, my friend, the thought brings the deed, she gives a quick glance around, no one to watch her. They are all still in the church, sheltering from the weather, or walking by the sea and so she pushes and nudges the stone pillar until it is in the right place and then gives it one last vigorous push, shuts her eyes, and runs away. She would, you see, my friend, in her own mind, bear no responsibility for the death. She would say to herself, "Well, all that I did was to give that pretty little stone angel a small thrust. I didn't realize that the hill was so steep and that it might do some damage. Not my fault! Just a pure accident! Nothing I can do! That man is undoubtedly dead!"'

Dickens sat back with an air of astonishment and looked across at me with a smile before resuming. 'And so, Wilkie, she just walks away and blots out the picture of what really happens. Just the sort of thing that a woman would do. Bless my soul, Wilkie, you can take my word for it. I know women, have been studying them for years.'

And Dickens, with a triumphant intonation to his voice, poured himself some more whiskey and began to sip it, while eyeing my expression over the rim of his glass.

I had to smile. Serious and all as the matter was, I just could not resist it.

'You're a genius, Dick,' I said and knew that there was a genuine note of admiration in my voice.

'Well, you know what that Scottish fellow, Carlyle says, "Genius is an infinite capacity for taking pains". Don't quite believe in that myself. Taking pains helps, but you need to be born with some mother wit as well, don't you think?' Dickens brooded upon the matter while I turned over his lecture in my mind. It was, I thought, a possibility, though I didn't want at this time to confine the suspects to women – especially as, now, Georgina seemed to be the only woman with any motive.

Aloud, I said, 'You have quite a number of young men here among your guests and you have two young men among your servants, so don't you think it is more likely that a man, rather than a woman, would commit a violent crime like this?'

Dickens gave an impatient sigh. 'I've just been explaining to you that this wasn't a violent crime, it was a murder, yes, but a murder at about fifty yards distance. Even the most delicate of women, in my opinion, could close her eyes or walk away and pretend to herself that she had nothing what-soever to do with the deed. I'd reckon that she or even he, whosoever was the murderer, may not have even walked down that hill, but would have slipped back inside the churchyard gate and dodged through the graveyard, keeping herself or himself hidden by means of all those piously planted bushes. Easy enough to rejoin the crowd in the church, or else to wander off some distance away into the heart of the marsh.'

I bowed my head. Never any use to argue with Dickens and there was a certain amount of truth in what he said. And it brought another idea into my mind.

'You know, Dick,' I said, 'I think your point about the perpetrator of this deed being able to distance herself or himself from the deed would also make it likely that his nephews could be the ones who sent that stone down the hill. They struck me as having little confidence in themselves and being very much in awe of their uncle. Allowing that rounded slab of stone to roll down the hill and smash into a sleeping man took far less courage than confronting their uncle, face to face, with a weapon.'

'My point, precisely,' said Dickens, who always liked to be the one that put forward the ideas. 'Now we need to find out if they were missing from the church at any point – not that it would be any proof, as I imagine people were going in and out. It wasn't exactly the most comfortable of places.'

'One of the nephews was outside the church when we arrived,' I said.

'Which one?'

'I don't know; I wasn't close enough to see him properly,' I confessed. 'The police sergeant told me that every single one of your guests had admitted to having gone out of the church at one stage or another, either alone or with a companion, but mostly alone, while sheltering in the church. The snow, he was told, was so light, that it was almost more pleasant out-of-doors than in that damp, cold little church. Well, that was what was said to him by a couple of people that he had been interviewing.'

'I see.' Dickens was silent for a few minutes and then he shook his head with a rueful and slightly amused expression upon his face. 'It may be that this murder is doomed to be a mystery for evermore. Never mind, from evil may come great good.' He stared for a moment upon a picture upon the wall of the room which was always mine whenever I stayed with him. It was one of those pictures beloved by Dickens which told a little story and this one portrayed a father coming home, up his garden path, laden with parcels and two small children staring eagerly out of an upstairs window. Like all those kind of narrative pictures, it had a title beneath it and it was on those words that Dickens appeared to focus.

'Great Expectations' muttered Dickens. 'That's what I will name it. Good title, eh, Wilkie. What do you think?'

'What, the picture?' I gave it a cursory glance. Dickens, I thought, should be putting more of his mind to solving the problem instead of leaving it to be doomed a mystery for evermore.

'No,' he said. 'My new book. I've had such a good idea. These marshes, the convicts and the prison ship, the scream of a very young child, it's all coming to me. Going to be one of the best, if not *the* best of my books, you mark my words, Wilkie. *Great Expectations*. I hope to make a fortune out of it. Bit of luck for me, this affair, wasn't it?'

And then, to my immense surprise, Dickens got to his feet, raised a hand to me, and drifted towards the door, with a happy smile upon his lips. 'Happy Christmas, my friend!' he said, picking up a minute piece of thread from the floor and placing it carefully into the waste-paper bin under the desk.

'But the murder, Dick, what about the murder?' I asked. I could feel how my eyes were stretched, widely opened, and how my jaw, literally as well as figuratively, had dropped.

'Leave it, Wilkie,' he said gently. 'Leave it. It hasn't done anyone any harm. The man was a villain and he deserved to die. The murder has served its purpose.'

And then with a wave of the hand, more like a benediction than a gesture of farewell, Dickens left the room, shutting the door quietly behind him. He had, I knew, the important task of donning his Santa Claus costume and slipping presents into the stockings of any of his children who were still under the age of ten. Carrie, I knew, would be included and I guessed that she would be incandescent with excitement in the morning. What a pity that this murder had interfered with the happy and exciting Christmas which Dickens planned every year, with such care, and such attention to detail as to make sure of happy and colourful Christmas memories for his ten children. It was, I thought, unlike Dickens not to worry about the fact that, almost certainly, beneath this hospitable roof of his dwelt someone who had brutally murdered one of his guests. Was he not worried about his children, as well as his guests? Surely, he should be! Perhaps he was taking on too much – entertaining his guests, ensuring that they, his children and his staff, had a happy and a memorable Christmas and at the same time, he was, apparently, in the throes of giving birth to a new novel which would, in his own words, be the best that he had ever written.

I, as a friend and an admirer, would have to step in and help. I would say no more to Dickens himself, but when I had worked matters out, I would, perhaps, make sure that the man or woman would know of my suspicions and would agree, after a threat of disclosure, to instantly leave the house and country before I confided in the police. I told myself that there was no doubt that the victim had been an unpleasant, black-mailing villain and the chances were that his assassin would never reoffend.

But who was the assassin? Surely, by now, I could work it out. I knew everyone in the house, every one of Dickens' friends were of the same circle which I frequented. I had dined with them, visited the opera in their company and listened to lectures by their side. And if, in the case of some of the younger guests, I did not know them as well as that, nevertheless, they were friends of friends, or offspring of families who had been known to me for years.

I was feeling sleepy. A little too much to drink, I thought reproachfully, going across to open the window and allow some of the sharp frosty air into the room. Pat, the Irishman, seemed almost the most likely. Unlike the others, he had been alone at the church that afternoon, and presumably kept himself and his horses warm by walking, up and down, while the others huddled together in the small, cold church. But was brotherly love sufficient for a man to commit a murder that might relieve a younger sibling from danger of disclosure? And then there was Georgina. Now that was a very different matter. Georgina was frightened for herself, frightened that she was in debt, might even be put in prison for debt, as no one but herself was responsible for her debts. The threat of prison, I thought, would terrify a girl like Georgina, brought up in the lap of luxury. I shook my head, meditatively filled the washbasin from the matching jug and added some hot water from the kettle left standing by the fire. I would go to bed, I told myself, as, with my mind filled with images of the moorland and the convict ship, my subconscious mind would probably sift all solutions and I would wake up with a name upon my lips.

# THIRTEEN

I awoke with a start. The clock on the wall said eight thirty. A bell was ringing, shaken vigorously by some boy with heavy boots bounding up the staircase outside my door, shouting at the top of his half-broken voice, 'Happy Christmas, everybody! Rise and shine! Rise and shine!'

I jumped out of bed, pulled on my dressing gown, went to the cupboard and found the carefully wrapped Christmas present for Carrie and went straight up to the nursery. They were all awake, all of the children, all with Christmas stockings and to my immense gratitude, there was one for Carrie also! She hugged and kissed me and tucked my present under her arm, but then went back to comparing stockings with her little friend Plorn. They were obviously the best of friends and so I slipped away as they started to strip the paper from a new box of toys which the governess took from the top of the wardrobe. Even when I reached the bottom of the stairs, I could still hear their excited voices.

Church first and then, on return from church, a magnificent breakfast was Dickens' instruction to his guests. I didn't fancy the church bit, though I was looking forward to the magnificent breakfast. I dressed slowly and reluctantly. I would, I suppose, be eventually compelled to make the effort, but I couldn't see why I should bother. I never attended church of my own volition and I certainly did not feel that I needed to do so to fulfil Dickens' ideas about a happy, fairytale Christmas.

Nevertheless, I dressed and went downstairs. Much easier to be there when they departed. Dickens was fully capable of counting his guests and sending an urgent messenger to rouse me from my sleep.

There was, considering the hour, a surprisingly good crowd of guests, many yawning ostentatiously, but all accepting a small bouquet or buttonhole of holly berries artistically bound to a few glossy, green ivy leaves. I took mine from Sydney and stuck it immediately into my jacket, searching my mind for some illness which might just appear when we were on the road to the church, not too far from Gad's Hill, but far enough to put any remedies out of the question.

But then I saw Jas Morehouse and one look at his face made me feel that he was in no way fit for that walk to church, nor was he fit to undergo any kneeling and standing and sitting on a hard and most uncomfortable wooden seat. In fact, all that he looked fit for was to go back to bed. I went straight to Dickens.

'Jas is not fit for this, Dick,' I said urgently. 'Let me take him back to his bedroom, get him something to drink and then if he insists, I'll get Pat or his brother to get out one of the horses and drive him to church.'

I thought that I would mention that, but Dickens, kind fellow that he was, shook his head. 'No, I think that he should lie upon his bed. Will you stay with him, Collins, if you would not mind? He doesn't look well; I should have noticed. He should not go to church today.'

I left him rapidly and went to stand by Jas. The guests and family members were forming into groups and pairs. Dickens gave one hasty look back at Jas's white face and then gave me a quick nod. I nodded back, put a hand upon Jas's arm and said quietly, 'Just sit down for a few minutes, old chap.'

He did so without argument. I guessed that he was reaching the end of his tether. I saw how he slipped his hand inside his jacket as though he had a pain in his chest. His face was white with a few beads of perspiration glinting upon it and one hand clasped his right arm, just above the elbow. I changed my mind about taking him back up to his room and just waited beside him quietly. The crowd of merry guests were streaming out towards the front door, gaily greeting each other, laughing and admiring the presents which Dickens' children were, by his instructions, reluctantly piling upon the hall table. One or two small items, including a very realistic rubber mouse, I noticed, were hastily stored within pockets and after a few minutes all had left the room. Through the window I watched them steaming down the path on their way to the road, the governess with a tight grip on both of her charges' hands as Carrie and little Plorn skipped along, singing merrily.

But when I looked back at Jas, I got a shock. He had sunk down upon a chair, not an easy chair but an upright, high-seated, hard-backed chair with no arms. One hand clasped the edge of the table beside him and for a moment I wondered whether to ring for assistance, but then as I looked out of the window and saw the stream of kitchen staff joining the procession, I guessed that I might, at least for the next ten minutes or so, be the only one left in the house. The kitchen staff, I knew, had gone to the early service and would soon be returning, but they might not be back in the house very quickly as they would be greeting all fellow staff and members of the house with shouts of 'Happy Christmas!' The children would be relating to the servants their booty from Santa Claus, (certainly all of these children regarded them as members of their families), the adults of the house and the guests also would be slipping a piece of silver into the hands of those who had worked to make their stay such a pleasant one. It would, I thought, be a good twenty minutes before I could expect any help.

But, in the meantime, I was alone with a man who looked very ill indeed.

And typical of Jas, his immediate thought was for me.

'Don't worry, Wilkie,' he said, his words almost inaudible. Then he added, with a tremendous effort, 'A bit better. Soon be well, old friend.'

But the grey pallor of his skin, and the thread-like utterance of the words, belied his efforts. The man, I thought, with a heartrending rush of anxiety, might well be dying. And I, Wilkie Collins, a scribbler of stories, had no idea of what to do for him. Dickens' house stood far from the nearest neighbour. In any case, I reckoned that most of the parish was, by now, kneeling in church with heads bowed. I would have to do my feeble best.

And there was another issue.

What could I say to a dying man?

Could I possibly open the subject which had occupied my mind during much of the last twenty-four hours?

But, if I did not, what terrible consequence could ensue? I opened my mouth and then closed it again. Another few minutes, wait another few minutes until he is stronger, I told myself, like the coward that I always was.

But it was Jas who started the conversation. After the few minutes had passed, he was, indeed, looking better. He sat very straight, very silently, looking first towards the window and then towards the clock upon the wall. It struck the half-hour and we both gazed at it and waited until all was silent again. And when he spoke, I could hear that an element of strength had come back into his voice.

'Last will and testament, old boy,' he said and straightened his back, looking intently at me. A minute of silence ensued while I looked back at him and he, poor fellow, sat visibly gathering his strength. And somehow, I guessed what was in his mind. What I had to do now, I told myself, was to make matters easy for him. I had a strong feeling that we shared thoughts and even while I considered this possibility, gazing at him uncomfortably, he bowed his head.

'Yes,' he said, 'I thought that you knew, Wilkie. How did you guess?'

'Process of elimination,' I said, relieved that he had broken the silence. 'Georgina had told you, her story; I guessed that when I saw the two of you together, saw you comforting her. You heard her story, you may have heard others, almost certainly a generous man like you would have rescued your nephew and so you knew what misery the man had caused. And,' I finished, 'you are a man of courage, a man who takes responsibility for others upon your shoulders.'

Another moment of silence passed as he looked intently at me, and I looked back at him. Then I broke the silence. 'And, of course, one of the convicts saw you later, he saw you from the ship. He told me that. Saw you with Georgina first and then alone.'

He smiled a little ruefully. 'And there was I checking that the bell had sounded and that all of the convicts had disappeared below deck for their midday meal – at least I hoped it was for a midday meal, poor creatures.'

It was like him, I thought, to worry about the convicts and whether they were given a midday meal. However, right now I was warned by his appearance as he looked extremely ill. There were beads of perspiration upon his forehead, his voice was weak and I could see how his hands trembled. If the secret was to be told to a witness, not long remained.

'What happened?' I asked as gently as I could.

'I felt uneasy and worried,' he said slowly. 'I had been wondering what to do. I could save my nephew who might otherwise end up in a debtor's prison, I might even be able to manage a loan for Georgina, but what about all the others who were tormented and swindled, as my nephew was, by this evil man. And then I saw him, saw that dastardly man who was causing such unhappiness and might even be responsible for many suicides – I knew of one at least, though little had been said about it . . .'

'And so you saw him, on the hillside, was it?' Gently I brought him back to the subject. There might not be much time left. I needed to know what had happened yesterday.

'I thought he might have hurt himself,' said Jas said in a low voice. 'I even, for one moment, hoped that he might have had a stroke or a heart attack, but no, as I came to the top of the hill, I could hear him snoring loudly. The man was drunk and not surprising given the amount that he had swallowed of Dickens' wine. I wished, I remember, that he had tripped and split his skull, but no, those snores were regular and healthy.'

Jas stopped for a moment, staring ahead of him, nursing his strength, I thought, and silently I poured a glass of water from a side table and brought it across to him. He tried to smile, but his face was set in lines of deep sorrow and anxiety. It would be thus, I thought, that a man goes to face his maker. He read my thoughts and with an effort smiled at me, a wry, and self-conscious smile. 'It was a wise man who said, "For evil to flourish, it only requires a good man to do nothing",' he uttered quietly and added, 'or so I told myself.'

He paused for a moment, slowly rubbing his left arm as

though it pained him intolerably and then, appearing to make a strong effort, he resumed. 'It just came to me, Wilkie. I thought that if a stone tumbled down the hillside it might knock the brains from the head of that abominable man. And, believe it or not, after what seemed like only moments, I came to a decision. I found myself moving stones, opening an exit on the wall above and then with a single hard push, one of those angels was rolling down the hill. Stupidly, and child-like, I must confess to shutting my eyes for a moment, and I prayed to God with an intensity which I had not used since I was a child, and I said, "In your hands, O God! I place this weapon." And then, Wilkie, I thought that God had done everything for me because a terrible pain struck me, here in my chest. I was convinced that I was going to die. I fell to the ground, drenched in sweat but managed to raise my head for long enough to know that the deed was done.'

Jas stopped, and it was another minute before he managed to say in a low tone, 'An evil had gone from the world, and I knew that God would exact payment, but that he would, when I had paid, he would forgive my sin,' he said simply, but with such confidence that I was happy for him.

And then, of course, as I would have expected from this man, he thought of others. With a huge effort, his face contorted with pain, his mouth wide open as he gasped for breath, he fumbled in his pocket and produced a pill. He was beyond speech, but I knew what he wanted and I took the pill and put it as far back into his mouth as possible and held the glass of water tilted so that he could drink from it.

The house was silent, and I held my breath. For a few moments I thought that nothing was going to happen, but then I saw him lift his head slightly. His lips were pale, but I saw them open as though he pulled in some life-giving air and then his back seemed to straighten, very slightly, but the sign was good. I released my breath on a sigh of relief. I saw him lift a hand, hold it out in front of him as though to examine, or even to calculate the time that was left to him. His eyes went to the table by the door. As always, Dickens made provision for anyone who wished to write a note, a poem, a song, or experiment with a new chapter or opening to a book. A small stack of paper was there. He was not capable of speech, but I knew what he wanted and guessed what he hoped to achieve.

I walked across to the table, came back with a sheet of paper, a pen and a bottle of ink. I sat down with the paper upon my knee, supported upon a book taken from the table. He nodded approval and then appeared to make a huge effort, sitting up a little straighter and drawing in a long, slow breath. This time it was he who took another pill from his pocket and this time he was able to lift the glass himself and swallow the pill. He waited for a moment, his eyes were widely open, not looking at me, but seemingly looking inward, assessing how much strength that he had left in his body.

And then he began to dictate in a hoarse and breathless voice, the words issuing so slowly from his colourless lips that I could easily keep pace with him.

'I, James Benedict Morehouse, now in the face of death, do solemnly make this last confession. I confess that I was the person who killed the man, named Timothy O'Connor, for reasons which will be known to my Maker. May God have mercy upon my soul!'

And then he stretched forward a trembling hand and I put the pen within it. I had an impulse to place my hand over his, thumb to thumb, but he shook it aside. A sudden rush of strength seemed to come upon him, and he signed the confession with a fluency and speed that I would not have credited minutes earlier, sitting back and fixing his eyes upon the ceiling, his face intent, his skin parchment white and his hands twisting over each other as though in the grip of a sudden and savage pain. I waited beside him, the signed confession in my hand and my eyes upon him. 'Watch and pray' were the words said to the disciples and that was all that I could do for him in this terrible extremity.

And it did not take long. An even deeper pallor came over his face and a sudden stillness upon his limbs. By the time that the first of the churchgoers returned, I had composed the body and locked the door to the library. The signed sheet of paper I placed inside my case and once I had locked it, I placed the key in the inner pocket of my waistcoat. It would, of course, have to be handed to the police, but not until Christmas was over.

Time for these affairs to be dealt with once the man had been suitably mourned and the Christmas celebrations had finished.

# EPILOGUE

When I looked back upon that Christmas Day, I was amazed to remember how smoothly everything went. The children's excitement helped immensely. And by an unspoken agreement, every adult in the house wanted to make sure that nothing was said or implied which might damage the memories of a day of such importance to them.

The body was removed while Dickens' daughter Mamie held a singsong in the schoolroom and by the time that the splendid lunch was served to all, there was a smile on every face as the new tradition of cracker-pulling began. Small presents, printed jokes and scented sweets spilled over the table. I think all the adults present silently thanked the memory of Tom Smith and his wonderful invention of these Christmas crackers which brought such excitement to the Christmas dinner table. The children's voices rose higher and more excited as the crackers exploded and even the most sedate of adults donned colourful paper hats and blew shrill whistles. The ladies oohed and ahhed over the small articles of artificial jewellery and there was much good-natured swopping of presents. Carrie had found a tin brooch in her half of a cracker and to the amusement of all she insisted upon pinning it to the lapel of my jacket. As soon as her back was turned, I passed it to Georgina and under the guise of pinning it to her scarf, I whispered in her ear, 'All is well.' I knew that she would have a happy surprise when Jas's will was read.

Almost a year has gone by, and Carrie is already dropping hints about her choices for Christmas. She had, it seemed, retained the happiest memories from her stay at Gad's Hill and no recollections of the death of the moneylender, Timmy O'Connor.

Jas's nephew made use of his legacy and reformed his way of life; Georgina, to her great surprise, had also benefited from Jas's will and this had been enough to set her on a new path.

The police were discrete about Jas's confession and the newspapers rapidly found new and more interesting stories, the least of which was the publication of Charles Dickens' new novel, *Great Expectations*, to tremendous critical acclaim.

# AUTHOR'S HISTORICAL NOTE

This book, I suppose, has its origins in the early 1940s when I first read, as a young child, Charles Dickens' famous novel *Great Expectations*. The book terrified but fascinated me, especially the graveyard scene. And in the ensuing almost eighty years I have gone back to it again and again. I have often wondered how much Dickens was influenced by the strange little churchyard, Cooling churchyard, and whether perhaps, as in my book, the presence of a convict triggered the plot of his famous story. In my opinion, it is one of his greatest, if not *the* greatest of his books.

He, on one of his long walks, would have seen the work done by the convicts, in deepening and widening the Medway estuary, and seen how they were housed in the hulks. It is also possible that he might have witnessed an attempted escape from one of those hulks.

Dickens himself had a guilty secret. He never, during their long friendship, disclosed to Wilkie Collins, that he had been brought up as a poor boy who worked in a blacking factory, while his father served a prison sentence for debt. It is this element of his childhood that I have used in the scene where O'Connor mentions the address of a blacking factory in their parlour memory game.

Dickens, due to his genius, ended up a wealthy man in his later years, and in this book, I have tried to convey his sense of conviviality and the extent of his large social circle of friends, which was very much enhanced by the fact that he loved to entertain them in his country house of Gad's Hill. Although Jas and the O'Connors are fictional characters, I have included many who were Dickens' real friends.

Arthur Sullivan's operas are still performed.

Daniel Maclise's pictures still hang in many art galleries, especially in his native city of Cork.

Wilkie Collins, ten years younger than Dickens, was a life-long friend and successful novelist in his own right.

Hablot Knight Browne was Dickens' illustrator and often holidayed with Dickens and his family.